Only One Bed

ONLY ONE BED

ISBN 979-8992273403

First Edition: January 2025
www.katiwilde.com

No Artificial Intelligence

No AI-generated content was used in this book's creation, including the storyline and text. This author has given no permissions and offers no rights for the contents of this book to be used to facilitate AI learning. These permissions and rights will never be given during the lifetime of the author and duration of the copyright. This book's copyrighted contents MAY NOT be included in any artificial intelligence content pool.

Content Warnings

Off-page but mentioned: Death of a parent due to vehicular accident (~twenty years in the past), parental infidelity and abandonment (~twenty years in the past), childhood emotional neglect by remaining parents, a stepparent making sexual overtures toward an adult stepchild, an adult sibling whose constant criticisms and negativity become an emotional and mental beatdown, adult family members taking advantage of familial bonds to exploit another adult family member's goodwill and financial/living situation, hypocritical do-gooders and do-nothings, and people who are generally lacking in kindness and/or compassion.

On-page: Snowmobile accident with minor injuries and mild concussion (the wreck is off-page, the injuries are not), taking an unprescribed dose of over-the-counter ibuprofen (800mg instead of the label's 400mg), seeking escape from an unbearable home life, swearing and vulgar language, the use of recently expired condoms, explicit heterosexual sex between two consenting adults, dubcon/noncon contact while sleeping (at one point, the hero and heroine unknowingly turn toward each other and snuggle. The slumbering heroine also rubs her genitals against the hero's; the hero is awake but doesn't halt the contact. Probably exactly what you'd expect in a book called Only One Bed).

The Dead Lands

(Discreet Cover Editions)
THE MIDWINTER BRIDE
THREE DEAD LAND BRIDES

(Original Covers & Ebooks)
THE MIDWINTER MAIL-ORDER BRIDE
THE MIDNIGHT BRIDE
PRETTY BRIDE
THE STONEHEART BRIDE
THE MIDSUMMER BRIDE
THE HARVEST BRIDE

Wolfkin & Berserkers
BEAUTY IN SPRING
HIGH MOON
TEACHER'S PET WOLF
SHERIFF'S BAD BEAR

Contemporary Romance
GOING NOWHERE FAST[1]
THE KING'S HORRIBLE BRIDE

Fantasy Romance
EVIL TWIN[2]

---

[1] Includes cameos by the Hellfire Riders
[2] Set in the same world as the Dead Lands

KATI WILDE

*Season's greetings to everyone
(except my cheating husband)*

INSIDE THE CABIN

Abbie

"THIS IS GOING TO BE THE BEST CHRISTMAS *EVER*," I DECLARE. My fingers, already aching after three hours of white-knuckling the steering wheel, tightly grip the wheel again when my chained tires jerk over a rut hidden beneath the snow.

Hot Biscuit Slim—never the jolliest cat to begin with—yowls mournfully from his carrier on the passenger seat. No doubt he's lamenting the day I fell in love with his grumpy little face and wishing himself back at the rescue shelter.

"It *is* going to be the best Christmas ever. And we *aren't* going to die," I mutter the last part forcibly, as if speaking the words aloud will prevent our likely imminent death on this narrow forest road.

At least, I *hope* I'm on the road. Rapidly falling snow has completely obscured the ground. I lost cell reception two hours ago, my GPS gave up any pretense of knowing where to go when I turned off onto the first, slightly less narrow forest road a few miles back, and my sense of navigation is reduced to 'try not to hit any trees.'

When a low-hanging branch burdened with snow scrapes across the side of my car, I amend that to 'try not to hit any tree *trunks*.'

Hot Biscuit Slim yowls again.

"Oh, hush! The weather app said it wasn't supposed to begin snowing until tonight. This is not my fault!"

The stink that suddenly erupts from the cat says he heartily disagrees. Frantically I roll down my window—and I'm hit with a wave of sheer mountain bliss. My lungs fill with clean, crisp air. Only a degree below freezing, it isn't bitterly cold but delightfully refreshing. Fat flakes drift downward, so soft and quiet and lovely that for an instant, the painful tension of hunching over my steering wheel while trying to navigate an increasingly treacherous road eases from my back and shoulders. Then a branch overhead releases a giant glop of wet snow that bombs the edge of my open window and explodes. By the time I brush the worst of it off my lap, icy water has soaked my crotch.

Hunching over the steering wheel again, I grind out from between gritted teeth, "Best. Christmas. Ever."

FIFTEEN MINUTES LATER, HARRIS'S CABIN pops out of nowhere. One moment I'm crawling along with trees to either side of me, the next moment a clearing opens up and the road ends. Squatting beneath the tall firs is the log cabin where I plan to spend the next two weeks. I'll give myself a perfect Christmas, the kind I've always dreamed of—which ought to be easy, since I'll be alone.

Almost alone.

My spiteful ball of claws and orange fur growls menacingly as I lug his carrier through the snow to the tiny covered porch. After fumbling with the key ring in my gloved fingers, I open the padlock that secures the door to the frame, then the deadbolt. Cold, stale air greets me when I push inside.

My heart gives a happy skip. Though the shuttered windows allow in barely any light, what I can see of the interior is exactly as Harris described. Aside from the closet-sized bathroom, the cabin is laid out as a single large room. A queen bed is shoved into the far corner with a chest of drawers at its foot. To my right, two oversized leather armchairs face a stone fireplace. In the center of the cabin sits a round table with two wooden seats tucked underneath; a kitchenette and cabinets fill the wall to the left. Altogether, it isn't much bigger than my first studio apartment was, so I feel right at home.

Despite the exhaustion of my harrowing drive, renewed energy surges through me. I pull out Harris's instructions, then go around igniting the pilot lights for the fridge, stove, and water heater. I find a snow shovel in the shed behind the cabin, clear the short path to my car, and begin unloading my bags and boxes. My efforts are accompanied by the merry sounds of Hot Biscuit Slim yowling in the bathroom, where I'd locked him in with his litter. The last thing I need is for him to escape through the front door while I'm carrying everything in. Undoubtedly he'd scamper out into the forest—forcing me to chase after him, probably only to get lost and freeze to death. Meanwhile, he'd scamper back to the cabin, tear his way into my Christmas ham, and not miss me one bit.

This is what I get for being charmed by a cute, grumpy face. But at least I'm not susceptible to a handsome face. I was vaccinated at an early age against that particular condition, courtesy of John and Reed Knowles—a father and son who might be the most beautiful men I've ever seen but who are also vengeful bullies and lawless cheats. Now I'm utterly immune to chiseled good looks.

They're also the reason I'm hiding out here in my boss's cabin, desperate to be alone, instead of spending the holidays at my own home.

Ugh. Why am I thinking about the Knowles? Those assholes don't deserve to take up space in my head. And they definitely don't have any place in the best Christmas ever.

Deliberately I shove them from my mind—along with all the horrible history that they represent—and start unpacking.

I WAKE UP THE NEXT morning with fifteen pounds of feline disdain sitting on my chest and his right front paw smashing the center of my tit. Never would I accuse a cat of hurting me deliberately, but holy shit—it's like he *knows* where the most painful place to step is.

Cursing, I push him off and roll out of bed. I instantly

wish I'd had the forethought to lay out my slipper socks and fuzzy robe before I went to sleep. The cabin is *freezing*. But wearing any kind of pants or socks in bed drives me crazy, so I dance around on the frigid floorboards in my panties and flannel pajama top while I dig through the suitcase sitting atop the chest of drawers. My toes are nearly ice by the time I yank on a pair of fleece socks, then hurriedly drag on the flannel pants that match the top.

It's slightly warmer near the fireplace, where embers remain from last night's fire. I toss in a few pieces of wood, then stand there shivering with my hands tucked inside my sleeves and my arms wrapped around my chest. Hot Biscuit Slim winds his way between my feet, meowing for his breakfast.

My brain thaws out a few minutes after my toes do. I fill his dish, then check my phone out of habit.

No messages. Because, of course, no cell service. The cabin is completely off the grid.

And it's only 4:54 A.M.

That effing cat.

I give Hot Biscuit Slim a look of disgust. Not that he cares. And I suppose that even though he woke me up early, I also went to bed far earlier than usual—around eight o'clock. So I've had a full night's sleep and might as well get a jump on the day.

It's strange not to begin the morning on my computer or my phone. Usually I have coffee at my desk, not curled up in an armchair in front of a fire. Weird, but nice to just sit and take stock of everything I need to get done today.

First will be removing the padlocks from all of the window shutters so that I won't have to use my battery-powered lanterns during the day. Second will be to finish unpacking—although, since it's still dark outside and will be for a few more hours, maybe unpacking should come first. Yesterday, my surge of energy lasted long enough to bring in everything from the car, but I only managed to put away my groceries before I crashed.

Once all that is done, I can start on my third—and most anticipated—item on the to-do list: hunting down a Christmas tree. Normally I wouldn't go traipsing out into the forest alone, because I'd have a one hundred percent chance of getting lost. I won't worry about that today. The snow stopped soon after I arrived but won't melt anytime soon, and my tracks will leave a clear path for me to follow on my way back to the cabin.

So as soon as I finish items one and two on my list, I'll unleash my inner Paul Bunyan and go get me a tree.

I'M UNLOCKING THE LAST SHUTTER when the wind suddenly picks up and the temperature drops. For a few seconds, I think about going to look for a tree anyway. The icy burn against my face persuades me to head back inside.

Christmas is still four days away, so there's no rush. Instead of playing lumberjack, I can decorate the cabin or start on a new painting while waiting for the weather to clear. And even if I never get a tree, this *will* be the best

Christmas ever.

But then, just about any Christmas would be better than another year spent with my mom and my sister.

That thought immediately makes me feel guilty. Then angry for feeling guilty. Neither emotion is what I want to feel, so I get out my portable Bluetooth speaker, load up Mariah's *Merry Christmas* album, and sing along at the top of my lungs while aggressively threading a popcorn garland.

The next time I glance through the windows, there's nothing but white. Not softly swirling white, either, but rushing sideways and driven by wind that—as soon as I pause Mariah—whistles and howls. I can barely see my car, though it's parked only three feet from the porch.

"Holy shit," I breathe, holding the plaid curtain aside. "Do you see this?"

Curled up sleeping in front of the fireplace, Hot Biscuit Slim doesn't even lift his head. I stand there for a few minutes more, staring in wonder at a blizzard unlike any I've seen before. All the while, in the back of my mind I'm turning over any possible problems the storm could cause.

Electricity isn't an issue. The well pump runs on solar, which should have enough juice in the batteries to last a few days, even if I drip water to make sure the pipes don't freeze—and there's a small gasoline generator in the well house that serves as a backup. The appliances use propane, which has a full tank. I've got a battery pack to charge my devices. If that empties, I can recharge it in the car. Wood fills the log rack by the fireplace, with more stacked on the porch and beside the shed. And I brought a lot of food, far more than I need. Just in case.

Really, I could be snowed in for several weeks without much problem. The only real issue might be boredom. This is already the longest I've been unplugged from the internet or any streaming service in…I don't even know. A long time. But I knew I'd be off the grid, so I brought my paints and a few thrift-store canvases to work on—and if I finish those, I've got a ton of books downloaded to my phone. Even if my phone dies, Harris has paperbacks (all horror, *exactly* what someone needs to read while alone in the woods) tucked under the side table between the armchairs.

As long as I refrain from accidentally burning the cabin down, I should be fine for the duration of the storm—and however long it takes to dig myself out after.

But in all of the scenarios I pictured, of all the problems I considered, not once did I imagine someone would stagger out of the forest in the middle of a blizzard and pound on the cabin door.

Yet five minutes after I go to bed, that's exactly what happens.

Abbie

THE IDEA THAT SOMEONE MIGHT BE OUT IN THE BLIZZARD seems so impossible that for a few seconds, I sit up rigid in bed, wondering if what I heard was the wind knocking down a tree. Maybe the branches thumped against the cabin door? That would probably mean my car was smashed, too, but I never really liked how the seat's headrest makes it impossible to wear my hair in a claw clip anyway—

Thump, thump, THUMP!

Definitely someone pounding against the door. Maybe a shout, too, though over the storm it's impossible to know what they're yelling. But it's unmistakably a voice. Then the knob rattles, turning back and forth.

I scramble out of bed. Halfway across the room, I abruptly recall that I'm only wearing my flannel pajama top and underwear…and that I'm completely alone, and there's no way to call for help if the person outside is dangerous.

Maybe even a serial killer.

That thought freezes me in place, but I'm already right by the door. My heart thunders. What do I do? Put pants on, obviously, but that's the easy answer. Do I let this person in?

A gust of wind makes an eerie, hollow sound inside the chimney. I can't see anything through the small window that looks out over the porch, just my own faint reflection.

Thump, thump, THUMP!

I jump, then snatch the fireplace poker. Fear has dried out my mouth, and I have to work up enough saliva to shout, "Who is it?"

A male voice answers, though the words are muffled by the door and drowned by the storm. Probably yelling that he's freezing out there. That he'll die if I don't let him in.

My stomach knots. Anyone stranded outside tonight probably *will* die. To save him, I just need to open the door.

And really, would a serial killer be out in a storm like this? Surely a murderer would wait out a blizzard in a nearby town? It's not like I'm going anywhere and I could be killed just as easily *after* it stops snowing. It would be really stupid to come out here now to murder me…and surely I could outsmart anyone *that* foolish. Surely I could.

Okay, then. Whoever this is, I'll save him.

Clutching the poker, I flip the first deadbolt, then the second. The door crashes inward so fast, I stumble back to avoid getting hit. A giant abominable snowman bursts through on an icy blast of wind—completely covered in white, from his enormous boots to the fur-lined hood that partially obscures his face. He slams the door closed by falling back against it, pushes up the ski goggles masking his eyes, and suddenly I'm staring at someone I *wish* I didn't recognize.

Not an abominable snowman. Just abominable.

Fucking Reed *Knowles*. Why did I let him in? *Why?*

I should have let him freeze.

He blinks hard when he gets a good look at me standing in the light of the fire, glowering at him and holding the poker like a baseball bat. His gaze darts around the dim interior of the cabin—probably looking for Harris—before coming back to me.

Still glowering. Still ready to bash his head in.

"*You.*" He spits that word like a curse. "You're one of the Walker girls. The vicious one."

He's just saying that because I bit him once. Right on the meaty part of his hand, hard enough to draw blood. I don't know if he has a scar. I hope so.

"I'm only vicious when there's a reason." I give the poker a waggle, daring him to give me a reason. It doesn't even need to be a good reason. "Why are you here?"

His eyes narrow. "I've got a blanket invitation from Harris."

Harris O'Neil. My boss. His friend.

I like Harris, and I usually like his friends. Not this one. "Don't you check with him before using that blanket invitation?"

"Usually do." A muscle in his jaw works. "Didn't tonight."

"You should have. Because I'm here until after the new year, which I *did* clear with him. That means I've got first dibs, and I'm not going. So you're leaving," I say, and he tugs off his gloves. As if declaring his intention to stay even before he replies—

"Can't."

Apparently he also can't be bothered to speak in complete sentences anymore. "Yeah, you can. You just"—letting go of the poker with one hand, I make a flitting gesture toward the door, which he's still leaning against—"go back the same way you came. How *did* you get here?" I would have noticed lights from a vehicle, even in a blizzard.

"Snowmobile."

"Then you can snowmobile away."

"Wish I could." His words seem to slur together and his big body sags against the door. "Listen—"

That comes out more like *lissssen*. "Are you drunk?"

I can't smell anything on him. But now that I'm paying attention, he doesn't look too steady and his speech is definitely impaired.

He gives his head a shake—then winces as if the motion hurts and closes his eyes. "No. Though I had an accident—"

Outrage shoots through my veins. "While driving drunk?"

"*No,*" he bites out, and the force of that denial seems to pain him, too. Reaching up, he pushes his hood back and touches his head—and when he brings his hand forward again, blood coats his fingers. Blood that he doesn't see, because his eyes are still closed. "And before your goody-goody Walker brain decides to find something else to accuse me of, I wasn't running off with someone's wife, either."

That nasty jab obliterates the small amount of sympathy I felt at the sight of his blood. "Let me guess—someone shot you? Can't say I blame them."

Reed doesn't respond to that. Instead he blinks at his bloody fingers, as if surprised by his own injury. "A tree branch came down on me."

A big one, I'd guess. Probably broke under the weight of the snow. Too bad it didn't knock him senseless.

Or maybe it did. Because his back starts sliding down the door as if his legs aren't supporting him anymore.

"Oh, no no no no—you can't do that here!" I drop the poker and grab hold of his shoulders, trying to keep him upright. Not easy, considering that he's a freaking giant. "We've got no cell service and my car's buried in snow. So you cannot pass out here, because I've got no way to help you if you've got a concussion. Or worse. And you *cannot* die. Not here."

"But I can die somewhere else?" He huffs out something like a laugh. "Better to die here. Your fingerprints are all over that poker and my skull is cracked open. Might be worth it to see another Walker get what's coming to them."

Something in me goes colder than the blizzard outside. "You think my dad dying wasn't enough?"

"Considering my mother's dead, too? No."

Asshole. But I should have known what his answer would be. Eighteen years ago, I was seven years old—and Reed was twelve—when my dad ran off with his mom. Before they got far, both were killed in a car crash. Though we've *all* paid enough, all grieved enough, the Knowles men will never stop persecuting my family. God knows why. Maybe because my dad wasn't available to punish, so the Knowles decided to take it out on the Walkers who were left.

He should have chosen a more tactful response, however, since I'm the one keeping him on his feet.

Not anymore. I let go of his shoulders.

Reed drops to the floor in a snowy heap. He lurches forward as if to get up—then seems to rethink that, sitting back again on his ass.

"Fuck," he mutters. "Fuck."

My thoughts exactly. "You are *ruining* my Christmas vacation."

"Not having a great time myself." He gives another of those short, huffing not-laughs. "What was already a shitty day has just gotten shittier."

I eye him warily, because he's got his arms draped over his upraised knees with his head hanging between them. "Are you going to puke?"

His throat works as he swallows once, then twice. Finally he says, "Not sure."

"Maybe you should be lying down?"

His grunt in reply sounds like agreement. Reluctant, but agreement. He doesn't make a move toward the bed, though.

I watch him for a long moment, struggling against my own reluctance. I don't *want* to help him. Anyone else in the world (excluding his father), I'd have already grabbed the first aid kit and started tending to the wound on his head.

I know what the right thing to do is. I never thought I'd be so slow to do it—and I hate myself for not taking the high road more readily. Reed Knowles is a garbage human being, no doubt. But I thought better of *myself*.

It's not as if I have to be nice to him, though. I just have to help him not die. Then he can get gone, and I can get back to having the best Christmas ever.

So I relent. Reluctantly. My heavy sigh as I give in to my better angels is probably more suited to a tantrum-throwing three year old, but I don't care. He already thinks I'm vicious—I'm not, normally, but I'll admit to making an exception with him—and what else did he call me? A goody-goody Walker? I'm not that, either, though my mom and sister try to be, in their own special ways. I also know that, four years ago, he cautioned Harris not to hire me, telling my boss that *"Those Walkers will throw shit in your face then say it was your own damn fault. They never take responsibility for the damage they do."* So a sullen sigh isn't going to make Reed Knowles think any less of me than he already does. And I don't give a damn about his opinion, either way.

"Can you make it to the bed under your own power?"

"Think so," Reed says, though he doesn't sound too sure.

"If you can't, we'll deal with it. But take off your coat and boots first, so you don't drip all over the floor." I switch on a battery-powered lantern and carry it into the bathroom where I stored the first aid kit. A passing glimpse in the mirror reminds me that I haven't put on pants yet—no biggie, since my pajama shirt hangs to mid-thigh—and that I also haven't taken a shower today, or done more than finger-comb my hair. Also no biggie, since Reed Knowles can kiss my unwashed ass.

In the short time I was gone, he managed to get his jacket off, but isn't doing so well with his snow boots. He's still sitting with his back against the door, but when he leans forward and reaches for the laces, his fingers fumble and pain hisses through his clenched teeth. After a moment Reed pauses, closes his eyes and leans back, then tries again. He fumbles and hisses and I can't take it anymore.

"I'll do it."

I bat his hands away from his snow-encrusted boots. My fingers are freezing by the time I dig through the layer of ice and loosen the laces, then end up falling on my ass when I haul his boot off his giant foot. *Of course* I land right on top of a melting glop of snow, and frigid water soaks through my underwear. Scrambling up into a crouch, I grab his left foot, lifting the boot from the floor. This time his sharp hiss of breath tells me that he might have injured more than his head.

"Is it your foot or your leg?"

"Leg." He gestures to the outside of his thigh.

I keep unlacing his boot, though more gingerly than before. "Another branch?"

"The same branch. It hit me, I blacked out. When I came to, I'd rammed the snowmobile up against a tree. I must have whacked my leg, though I don't remember doing it."

Ah, that's right. He'd said he had an accident. I can't

help needling him. "I guess you should've worn a helmet."

"I figured my head would be hard enough," he says, so dryly that I almost smile.

Almost. The day Reed Knowles makes me smile is surely the day hell freezes over. "Do you think you broke anything?"

"Only the snowmobile. I walked the rest of the way here. Probably couldn't do that if the bone was fractured." He grimaces as I slowly tug his boot free. "The muscle must be stiffening up now that I'm not moving."

I hope so. Anything worse, and there's no way to help him. "So I win, then."

"Win what?"

"I drove here *without* hitting a tree." Barely. "Can you stand?"

"We'll see."

He can, though not easily. Without putting any weight on his left leg and bracing his back against the door, he pushes up onto his feet. More snow splatters to the floor.

"Take off your pants first," I tell him. I sense that he'd normally have a smart-ass response to that, but his change in altitude and the pain in his leg have him fighting to remain upright instead of shooting off his mouth.

Sluggishly he unbuckles the first strap of the bib-style snow pants. The pants sag around his waist when he unbuckles the second strap. He pushes them down past his hips, but when he bends to shove them toward his feet, it's almost like watching the slow fall of a tree as his entire body begins to lean forward, all balance gone.

KATI WILDE

I rush in, hands flat against his chest, and shove him back upright against the door.

"Don't you *dare* fall," I snap, because he's so damn big that if he goes down, that's it. No way could I get him off the floor.

Eyes closed again, as if the room is spinning, he nods. "I don't think I ought to bend over again."

Well…shit. I clench my teeth in irritation, but really—there's not much choice here. I'll have to take off his pants myself.

But not until I'm sure he won't fall over. My palms are still flat against his chest, pressing him back against the door. "Are you steady?"

Reed nods, so I wait a few more seconds to make sure the head movement doesn't make him lose his balance again. Just long enough to become aware of the body heat coming through the thermal shirt he's wearing, and for some part of my brain to recognize how *solid* his chest is.

Probably because instead of flesh and blood—or a heart—it's full of concrete, lies, and the Knowles pride.

And the longer I stand there, holding him up, the more I think about what I need to do next. I don't want to bend over in front of his crotch while he's standing. Or worse, get on my knees. It makes my stomach roil just picturing myself in that position—a position that he can mock later.

I don't actually know that he *would* belittle me in such a disgusting way. None of the Knowles' vitriol toward my family has ever been sexual in nature, as far as I know. But

I can't bear the thought of giving him an opening for that kind of shit.

It's bad enough that he's going to end up in my bed.

After another moment's consideration, I figure out how to avoid crouching. Keeping my hands against his chest, I raise my left knee as high as I can—he's really freaking tall—so I can shove my toes down the sagging front of his pants and slide them downward. The base layer he's wearing underneath is smooth and tight, offering no resistance to the baggy snow pants. With barely any pressure, they crumple around his ankles.

"They're down," I tell him, anchoring the snow pants to the floor with my foot. "Can you step out without falling?"

He can. Slowly. And I guess he *does* have a heart—there's a deep and steady beat against my right palm. Probably pumping sewage through his veins.

"Ready to walk?" I ask him when he's free. "I'll stay next to you in case you need steadying."

He does need that steadying. Almost immediately he begins listing toward the fireplace.

"Hold up." I clutch his arm and try to steer him in the right direction. "We're going that way."

"Can't."

"Why?"

"Because there's only one bed." His voice is gruff, as if frustrated that he's been forced to point out the obvious.

"So?"

"So I'll sleep in a chair."

I don't know if he's trying to be chivalrous (though I doubt a Knowles man knows the meaning of the word, let alone has ever put chivalry into practice) or if he's afraid I'll jump his helpless bones the instant his back hits the mattress. Either way, the answer is the same. "Don't be ridiculous."

"I'm not—"

"You *are*. Your brain's been smashed and you aren't thinking clearly. But I am. So come on."

A few steps later he abruptly stops. "My pack." He reaches around to his back as if to check whether he's got one strapped to his shoulders. "Did I forget it?"

"You weren't carrying anything when you came in." And if he was so confused after the accident that he forgot his belongings, it's a miracle that he didn't get lost on his way to the cabin. "Is there anything critical in there?"

"Critical?"

"Like, I don't know—insulin? Other medicine?"

"No. Just clothes. And…work stuff."

There's no mistaking the worry on his face when he mentions his work. "Is your pack waterproof?"

His eyes close, as if in relief. "It is."

"Then unless your work appeals to bears, I can't imagine it's in any danger." We reach the bed, where I urge him to sit on the edge. "Don't lie down yet. I need to see if your scalp is still bleeding."

He tilts his head down, chin almost on his chest. I have to stand between his legs to get close enough to examine the wound. Anyone else, I'd have been thrilled to be cradled between those massive thighs. But this is Reed Knowles, so instead of admiring the way the thermals cling to his muscles or contemplating the size of his package, I'm only interested in his injury.

I find a cut and swelling on his crown. I smear in some antibiotic cream and hope that stops the bleeding. I've got gauze but, aside from wrapping up his entire head, I'm not sure how it'll stay on. His hair is too thick to stick a self-adhesive bandage in there.

"This cut isn't too bad, but I'm not sure what to do about this big lump," I say. "How's your leg?"

He shifts his leg and grimaces. "Hurts when I move it."

"Do you think you pulled a muscle or is it bruised?"

"Bruised."

"Then maybe we should put ice packs on your leg and your head? I really don't know. But people who are punched in the face always put a bag of peas on their cheek, yeah?"

"Yeah, they do." He sounds amused. "You have a bag of peas?"

I've got way better. I shove my feet into my boots and fill two quart-size food storage bags with snow from the porch. Tromping back inside, I tell him, "These will work for ice packs. I've also got ibuprofen—but listen. We've got nothing else. So you have to promise you won't die or let it get infected."

He gives me a scowling look of disbelief. As if I've just said something incredibly stupid. "That's not something I can promise. That's not something *anyone* can promise."

29

"Sure you can. You're just not trying hard enough. You will *not* ruin my Christmas."

"You said I was already ruining it. So maybe you're the one not trying hard enough. You don't seem very cheery to me."

"Oh, I *was* cheery. Before you arrived, I was having a jolly time—and I'm determined to have the best Christmas ever. I can't do that if you're dead." No, that's not right. "I can't do that if you're dead *and still here*. So you've got three days to get better and leave."

"Trust that I'm not hoping to stay."

"Trust that I don't give a flying fuck what you hope or feel." I give him one of the ice packs to use on his leg, then wrap the other in a hand towel and press it against the lump on his skull. Not hard, yet his breath hisses through his teeth. "Obviously."

Silence falls between us, with me standing there holding snow against his head while he presses the other bag to his thigh. The fire crackles, the wind howls, and I mentally tally up the number of extra blankets stored around the cabin. And...there's not enough. The plan I was beginning to form regarding our sleeping arrangements—which consisted of me curling up in an armchair—is simply not feasible. If we split the blankets, we'll both be cold.

Shit.

The clearing of his throat breaks through the quiet. Obviously he has something to say, but it takes a few more seconds before he finally spits it out.

"Thank you," says a Knowles man to a Walker woman.

Holy crap. It's a Christmas miracle. "You can thank me by leaving as soon as you're able to."

"*That* I can promise," he says.

Reed

So last night *wasn't* a nightmare. I hoped it was. But even before I open my eyes, the throbbing in my head and my leg tells me otherwise.

I'm really here, sharing Harris's cabin—sharing Harris's *bed*—with one of the Walker girls. Though I suppose she's one of the Walker women now. I went to the same high school as the older girl—*Laura? Laurel?* Hell if I remember. We weren't in the same grade, so she was easy to avoid. This girl, the younger sister, the red-haired one…I haven't seen her since the day she took a chunk out of my hand. She ought to have been easy to avoid, too—our city isn't big, but it's big enough that unless you've got the same circles of friends or work, you can go a long time without seeing someone you'd rather not. But my friend circle overlaps with her work circle, so Harris mentions her now and then.

I wish to fuck that he'd mentioned she'd be here at the

cabin. Maybe I wouldn't have left my dad's lodge last night. I'd have stayed there with his new family and pretended the shit with Karilee never happened.

But, no. I'm no good at pretending. And being snowed in with a Walker girl is better than staying in the same house as my new stepmother.

Marginally better.

From beside me, a curse comes out on a low groan. "Fuuuck. It wasn't a bad dream?"

Goddammit. Realizing that I wasn't stuck in a nightmare was my first thought on waking, too. My skull must have been whacked real fucking hard if my brain's on the same wavelength as a Walker's.

Not that I'll say it out loud. I decided last night, I'll be nice. No matter how the Walker woman provokes me, no matter how much acid drips from her tongue. She opened the door, then took care of me. Grudgingly, but she did. So I'll get along with her. Even if it kills me.

The way my head feels, it might.

She hisses. "Ouch, you little shit! Get off my tit."

What the fuck is she accusing me of? All my good intentions fly out the window. "My hands aren't anywhere near you, woman. I wouldn't touch Walker tit if you paid me."

"Aw, you won't? Golly-gosh darnit. That was item number one on my Christmas list: pay Reed Knowles to tiddle my tits. I guess I'll go cry pitiful tears in the bathroom."

It's too early and too dark to see anything, but her sarcasm is sharp enough to slice steel. She doesn't wait for my response. The mattress dips as she lurches over my body—I'm on the open side of the bed, while her side is pushed up against the wall, so *over me* is the only way off. Though she doesn't touch me, the jostling feels like a boot to my head and my thigh. The throbbing in both ramps up to a ten, hauling in some nausea and vertigo along with it.

The next few minutes aren't too clear.

There's more light the next time I open my eyes. She's built up the fire and is visibly shivering in front of it with a quilted throw wrapped around her shoulders. Beneath the small blanket is a thick red robe that reaches her knees, plaid flannel pajama pants, and fleece-lined socks decorated with snowflakes—rendering her petite form into a shapeless lump of fuzzy Christmas cheer, topped by an explosion of auburn curls that hang halfway down her back.

Yet my mind keeps lingering on the memory of how she appeared last night, all legs and curves and ferocity. My first thought upon seeing an unfamiliar woman in all her poker-wielding fury: *Harris, you lucky bastard.* But a glance around the cabin told me she was alone. No Harris. A second look at that wild red hair clued me in to her identity.

I'd been admiring a Walker girl.

That realization slammed into me harder than the tree branch. Hours later, lying in bed, I'm still feeling the effects. I'm trying to think about *anything* but the way she looked, eyes narrowed and wary, her full lips twisted in a snarl, small hands gripping that poker—silently daring the asshole who just stumbled into her cabin to take one wrong step.

What the fuck is wrong with me that I can't get that image out of my mind? Yet I can't focus on anything else. Not with the way my head is pounding. Worse than any hangover I've ever had. Worse than the shit I caught at the beginning of the pandemic. I don't think I'm sick with a virus now, but my whole damn body feels a lot like it did then, lethargic and weak, though I only banged my head and my leg.

"You should take these."

I don't know when I closed my eyes. But I must have, because I open them to find the Walker girl standing next to the bed, one arm extended toward me.

Sluggishly, I try to understand what she wants me to do. Shake her hand?

She makes an irritated little moue of her lips, no doubt biting back one of her acid comments before settling for, "You groaned. Like you were dying. It disturbed me."

"I'll try to keep my dying on the inside," I mutter, knowing I won't, because I'd rather disturb her. Especially if makes her do that pouty thing with her mouth. Then I spot the ibuprofen tablets lying in her palm. Either my vision is doubled or that's too many pills. "Four?"

In response to my blatant suspicion, she rolls her eyes. "I'm not trying to kill you. These are two hundred milligrams each. When I got my wisdom teeth out, they prescribed an eight hundred milligram dose. So I figure this is safe. Unless ibuprofen is bad for a concussion, but I can't look that up online right now." She shrugged. "I suppose it's a risk. Probably small. Depending on how shitty you feel, it might be worth taking."

A concussion. Right. That's the reason for the fog around my brain, muffling every thought except for how pretty she is.

No, not pretty. She's not that. She's…something else.

And I do feel shitty enough to take the risk. The room spins when I push myself up to sitting. I close my eyes until the world settles.

When I open them again, I freeze in place—staring at the foot of the bed. Not sure what I'm seeing. Some kind of furry orange gremlin.

"What the hell is that thing?" If there *is* anything. If it's not some concussion-induced hallucination.

Her eyebrows shoot upward. Her eyes crinkle at the corners and she bites her bottom lip—against a burst of hilarity, I realize, and suddenly I want to see her laugh. Want to hear it.

But that's the concussion talking. I'll play nice, but I have zero interest in seeing any Walker happy.

"That," she says, and there's a wobble to her voice as if her laughter is still right there on the tip of her tongue, "is the tit tiddler."

Tit tiddler? Oh fuck.

By the look in her eyes, she's enjoying how stupid I feel right now. My face grows hot, and I mumble an apology— completely inadequate, but all I can manage. I'm a fucking prick. I know it.

I can't meet her gaze. Not while embarrassment still

flushes my face. Even the tips of my ears are burning. I pretend they aren't, accept from her the pills and a glass of water, and study the cat as I swallow them.

Though obviously well-fed and clean, it's the most unfortunate-looking animal I've ever seen—a raggedy ginger with a squashed pug nose, whiskers resembling a drooping walrus mustache, and a sullen glower. "Was that thing in the cabin last night?"

Even with a concussion, I couldn't have missed seeing *that*.

"He hid under the bed when you barged in."

The cat doesn't seem afraid now. Instead he's staked his claim on her side of the mattress. After, apparently, staking his claim on her chest. The creature's baleful green gaze follows our movements when she takes back the empty glass.

I continue to eye him warily. "He doesn't look happy."

"He never looks happy. Are you up for food?"

Just the thought of chewing intensifies the throbbing in my head. "Maybe not yet."

"All right." She leaves my bedside and returns, dragging one of the chairs from under the small dining table. "In case you need to get to the bathroom and aren't steady on your feet yet. You can use it like a walker—and sit down on the seat if you become dizzy."

I want to say a crutch won't be necessary. But the way my head spins now and again, it might be. "That's…smart."

"Smart. Hmmm." She tilts her head, laughter sparking in her eyes again. I'm not sure yet what color they are. The light in this corner of the cabin isn't good enough. Some medium color. Hazel, I think. Maybe green. But whatever shade, her amusement seems to make her eyes brighten her entire face. "Did that hurt to say?"

"It did." But I have to admit, "Everything hurts right now."

"Hence the inner dying." She chews on the bottom corner of her lip, gaze running over me as if searching for anything else she can do to help, then shakes her head. "Well, let those pills kick in. Maybe you'll feel better soon."

AFTER A WHILE, I DO feel better. A little. Enough to convince myself that I can make it to the other side of the cabin without the use of the chair.

I do. Barely. I'm so damn shaky that as soon as I close the bathroom door behind me, I spend a good ten minutes sitting on the toilet lid, gearing myself up for the effort it'll take to stand again and piss. Not to mention the return trip to bed.

This is the most humiliating situation I've ever been in. But slightly less humiliating than if Harris found me dead outside his cabin door, since my keys are in my pack. Which is still strapped to the snowmobile.

He'd give me shit for that while standing over my frozen corpse. Then probably carve *Here Lieth One Stupid Fucker* on my gravestone.

The Walker girl saved me from that final indignity, at least.

I know better than to prod the lump on my head, but I get a look at my thigh when my pants are down. The bruise isn't too colorful yet. The green and purple are likely coming.

39

The whole area feels tender and hot, and every step hurts like a motherfucker.

But I don't want to lie in bed all day. So despite the pain, I carefully make my way to one of the armchairs in front of the fire. Seated at the table, the Walker girl watches me with a doubtful expression as I cross the cabin, then purses her lips when I manage the distance without falling flat on my face.

"Want coffee?" She taps the steaming mug in front of her, as if my rattled brain might have forgotten what coffee was. "Or water?"

I hate that she's still having to look after me. Even if my leg didn't hurt and my head didn't spin, I'm so shaky I can't trust myself to carry a full cup of anything.

"Water sounds good." So does coffee, but I don't know if the caffeine will be good for a concussion. And in order to heal, it's probably better to sleep than to artificially keep myself awake. "Thank—*ow, fuck!*"

Her cat jumps up onto my legs, with two paws and what seems like most of his weight landing squarely on my bruised thigh. Though I'm seeing stars and this goddamn close to crying, I gently urge him over to the other side of my lap.

The Walker girl arrives with my water, grimacing in something close to sympathy. "He always knows right where it hurts. Want me to move him?"

"He's all right." Curled up now like any cat, though still looking as friendly as a rabid bulldog. "What's his name?"

"Hot Biscuit Slim."

"Nothing about this cat is slim."

"And you're not a reed."

Fair point, but I'm not called Hot Biscuit Reed, either. "Did you make up that name or is it from something?"

"It's from something."

She doesn't volunteer *what* it's from. Though now that I'm thinking about it, I feel like I've heard the name before. I study the cat, trying to dig through the throbbing depths of my memory. Maybe something I read a long time ago? Or a cartoon character?

He looks like one. Like the animated version of a perpetually disappointed eighty-year-old man watching a bunch of screaming kids shit on his lawn. Fucking adorable.

The Walker woman is currently wearing the same grumpy expression. Not sure if it's adorable or terrifying. "He never cuddles on *my* lap."

Wordlessly I stroke my hand along his back. A soft purr fills the air.

She glowers at us both before spinning and returning to the table. Outside, the wind has eased up but the snow hasn't. There's not much light coming in through the window, so she's set up a small halogen lantern to illuminate a project she's got spread out. My gaze remains on her face for a while. The brighter light reveals a faint smattering of freckles that weren't as visible by firelight. In my bashed-head state, those freckles are fucking mesmerizing. As is the way her upper lip is a bit plumper and poutier than her lower one, which I didn't notice until I saw her in profile. Now I can't stop looking.

Although I'm watching her, it's a long time before I actually see what her hands are doing…which is viciously stabbing cranberries with a needle before shoving them onto a string.

"Are you making something or cooking?"

"Making." She impales another cranberry. "A garland for the tree."

"What tree?"

"The one I'll go out and get as soon as it stops snowing."

Which doesn't appear to be any time soon. "Any idea when it's supposed to?"

"If the ten-day forecast hasn't changed, it should stop today. Then there will be two clear days with temps around freezing. But it's supposed to warm up into the fifties on the 26th and stay warm."

Fuck. "Any rain? It'll melt the snow faster."

"Not much, if any."

"So I'll probably be stuck here until around New Year's." Because with the amount of snow being dumped, even with warmer temps and tire chains, it'll be a while before the road clears enough to drive.

"Yep."

The shortness of that reply tells me she's as thrilled as I am at the idea of being trapped in the same cabin for another week. Maybe even *less* thrilled, if the way she jabs the next berry is any indication.

But if I'm not leaving any time soon, I should probably

learn her name. "Which one are you?"

"Which what?"

"I know you're a Walker. I don't know which one you are."

She briefly pinches her bottom lip between her teeth and that top lip pillows out a little more. "Well," she says, "it depends on who you ask."

"What?"

"To *you*"—she casts her gaze briefly my way, arching her brows before turning back to her garland and skewering a berry through the gut—"I'm the vicious one."

My face feels hot again, which irritates the hell out of me. I'm not a blushing man. Yet the heat doesn't recede as she continues. It just sits there, under my skin.

"But to someone else I know, I'm the disappointing and ungrateful one—and the one who will never live up to my full potential. To someone else, I'm the scourge of the earth, a slave to capitalism and enemy to the downtrodden, as well as a traitor to all that's good and decent." She slants me another arch look. "Exactly which one of those depends on what day it is."

The flush in my face has spread all over now and gone beyond irritating, making everything in my field of vision waver like heated air over asphalt in summer. "I just want your name."

"Ah." She seems to consider. "No, I don't think so."

"What?" My brain's sluggish, but I think she just refused to tell me her name.

Who does that?

She gives an unconcerned shrug. "I don't feel like telling you."

I don't know what to say in reply. I stare at her, head pounding, leg aching, skin burning. Trying to fathom the sheer stubborn *senselessness* of being stuck in a one-room cabin with another person and not sharing your name with them.

After a while, the unreasonable woman asks in the most reasonable tone, "You hate us, but you don't even know our names?"

"I do my best not to think of any Walkers at all." Especially not while my brain is in a throbbing fucking fog. Though I know she's not Laurel or Laura. That's the one I went to school with. Lauren? Lauryn? That's it. *Lauryn.* I'm pretty sure. I remember the Y from somewhere. In a yearbook, maybe. Christ, that was a long time ago.

"I suppose you also do your best not to think about how to tear our lives apart?"

"I honestly haven't fantasized about that in a while."

She scoffs. "How long is a while? A year and a half ago? Because that's when you stole my mom's house out from under her. Remember? She said you were there. You and your dad."

Angela. That's her mom. That one, I'm certain of. I've seen her name too many times over the course of my life, in continuous lawsuits that all failed and on my business's social media accounts until I blocked her. And the last time I saw her...

"I wouldn't say we stole the house out from under her." But my head's too fucked to think about how I *should* say it. "I remember there was some tax trouble."

"Tax trouble?" She gives a short, disbelieving laugh. "As if your dad's cronies at the county didn't cause that trouble by reassessing the property value for far more than it's worth. Far more than anyone could reasonably pay, dismissing her appeals, then slapping her with a levy. And the man who bought it for nothing just *happened* to be your dad."

"Pretty sure it wasn't for nothing." Though I can't recall exactly how much it was.

"Your idea of nothing is a hell of a lot different from mine." Her glare sears me from across the cabin. "But the money was never the point, was it? She said your father *gloated* as the papers were signed. That he crowed about how he couldn't wait to bulldoze it all. How he couldn't wait to destroy everything my dad once loved."

My face is hot as fuck. And the heat's sinking in deeper and deeper. "He did gloat."

"But you didn't? Can you honestly say you weren't thrilled the Walkers were brought so low? Or that you weren't glad to see the home where my mom and sister lived razed to the ground? Last night you said you'd be happy if another Walker got what was coming to them. So tell me you didn't enjoy seeing my mom's house bulldozed."

"I can't." Not after all the shit that woman pulled. "I was even there to watch it happen."

My brain must be completely scrambled, because it

takes the widening of her eyes—as if even *she* is stunned that I'd admit to something so callous—to realize that maybe I should have held my tongue on that one. That I should have softened it. Especially since I'm at her mercy here. And she's been taking care of me.

Instead of grabbing up the poker and giving me another whack to the head, though, she merely sets her jaw and returns to stabbing berries.

I watch her, my gaze wandering over that lip, her freckles, then that hair. My mind wanders with it. Absently I rub the crescent scar below my thumb. Remembering the last time I saw this one. Even then, with wild red hair. The recollection is hazy. Mostly a memory of being shocked that she'd bitten me, and of the blood on the white dress shirt that I'd worn to the funeral home. And how my father was shouting at her mother, and her mother was screaming at my father, and her older sister was pulling her away and calling her—

"Abbie."

Her head jerks up and she stares at me, eyes wide. And I was right. Hazel.

"That's what it is. Yeah? Abbie."

Her jaw clenches. Her chin dips in a small nod.

I suppose she could have pretended I was wrong. Could have strung me along like she's stringing those berries, while holding onto whatever pleasure it'd given her to deny me in the first place. But I suspect this isn't a woman in the habit of lying. Or in the habit of saying anything but what she truly believes.

Abbie.

"I guess I'm thinking of you now," I tell her.

"Don't," she says, and returns to her decorations.

Don't. But I won't be able to help thinking of her. Won't be able to help looking at her, either. She's too…*pretty* is not the right description. Not when I think of her poker-wielding fury. Not when I think of how her eyes shoot fire. But I can't think of the right word to describe her.

That's not like me.

But the throbbing mist around my brain keeps closing in, and thinking hurts too much. Despite sleeping all night, the heat and the fog are dragging me down again.

It's too much effort to fight them.

Abbie

I'm not sorry that Reed stays quiet in one of the big armchairs all morning. Sleeping…or maybe he passed out. Not sure. He stirs around noon, just as I start thinking about lunch. Something that'll be easy on his stomach. Last night, he looked as if he might puke at any second. He didn't eat anything this morning, either. So best to make a meal that'll be as easy going down as it is coming up, just in case he can't *keep* it down.

Combined with the snow outside, seems like it's the perfect day for minestrone. And if it turns out Reed doesn't like soup…well, fuck him. He can eat it or he can starve. I don't care.

I pull out my knife and get started on the vegetables. Cooking is something I enjoy, though I haven't done it much lately. Not at home. But thinking of home and all the reasons I've preferred to eat at restaurants the past year and a half—to be *anywhere* but home the past eighteen months—makes my stomach fill with lead. Because this time in Harris's cabin is a godsend…but these two weeks won't last forever. Real life will intrude again. The voices of my mom and sister will intrude again, and they'll tell me I'm not making the minestrone right (as if there's one right way to make it), that I'm making too much (as if there's no such thing as leftovers), and that next time we should all agree on what to eat together (as if my vote would even matter.)

I *won't* think of them, though. Not now. I won't think of what awaits me when I return home. I'll just enjoy my time here, because even with a concussed Reed Knowles taking up a good portion of the air in this cabin, he's been less terrible than spending five minutes in their company is.

To be fair, though, he's been sleeping most of that time. He's just as horrible—or worse—when he's conscious. And, god help me, when he's *talking*.

He actually admitted to being glad that my mom's house was bulldozed. That he went to watch it happen. *Admitted it.* And waved off the underhanded way his dad got his hands on the property. It's no surprise the Knowles men are trash. But for fuck's sake. Reed had to realize that was also my childhood home. It doesn't matter that I got out of there the second I turned eighteen. He couldn't know that. So the indifferent manner of his admission was simply staggering.

Oh, and now my blood's up. But I will not commit murder. I won't.

But only because it's Christmas. And hiding a body is

not in my Yuletide plans.

I plonk bowls onto the table and yank a pair of crusty French rolls out of the oven (*not* baked by me; I enjoy cooking but my bread always has the density of a white dwarf star.) And, okay—the soup smells amazing, and the bread smells even more amazing—and somehow those two things take the sharpest edge off my anger.

This *will* be the best Christmas ever. It will. Even if only because of the food.

"Lunch is ready," I announce. Then because I'm not a monster—unlike a certain abominable asshole with the last name of Knowles—I grab his chair from beside the bed and return it to the table.

Though awake, Reed still seems half out of it when he lurches out of the armchair to join me. His leg obviously pains him. His breath hisses each time he puts weight on it—which he barely does. And though stubble covers most of his jaw, the rest of his face is flushed. At first I thought it was either from the effort of crossing the cabin or the heat from sitting in front of the fire, but even after he eases into his seat at the table, his cheekbones retain a reddish hue. Then there's his hand, which trembles while bringing the spoon to his lips.

He takes a bite and his gaze lifts to mine. I brace myself for whatever shit he's about to say.

"That's damn good."

Well, well, well. Christmas miracle number two. Three, if I count his mumbled tit-tiddler apology.

But I don't think I'll count that. As apologies go, it wasn't much of one.

I'll be polite, though. "Thank you." *Asshole.*

"Thank *you.* I know you don't have to. And don't want to." He glances toward the fridge while I'm still fighting the urge to declare how very much I *don't* want to. "Do you have enough food for both of us, however long this snow lasts?"

Does he think I wouldn't have enough sense to ration if I didn't have enough? Is the big man with the ouchy leg going to take charge here?

Eyes narrowed, I ask, "What are you going to do if I don't?"

"Go out and hunt a bear."

I stare at him. He can't be serious. But it's hard to tell. He doesn't return my stare. Instead he's calmly looking down at his bowl, tearing a bite from the roll and dipping it into his soup.

Maybe he *is* serious? His tone was even, as if hunting a bear was a completely normal thing to do. And he did whack his head pretty hard.

"A bear," I finally echo, keeping my tone as even as his was. "With what weapon, I wonder? Will you whittle a spear?"

"I'll just do it with my bare hands."

No. He did *not* just make that joke. I regard him in horror. There was no emphasis on *bare* and yet…his expression is bland, *too* bland. Then his mouth kicks up at one corner. God help me. He knew it was terrible, but he did it anyway.

But I'm not going to laugh. Or even smile. I'll never

give anyone named Knowles the satisfaction.

Despite that resolution, almost thirty seconds pass before I trust myself to speak without betraying how near I came to chortling. "Well, luckily for you—I brought enough food for both of us. More than enough."

"Glad to hear. I'll pay you back for the portion I eat," he says, suddenly grimacing. He reaches up toward his head.

"Don't," I say sharply. He stops and looks at me. "There's a lump, but there's also a cut. Wash your hands before you touch it. I suppose I should put on more antibiotic cream, too."

That's how I end up close to him again, though this time standing behind his chair instead of between his thighs. But still close enough to feel the heat radiating off his body as I dab the cream onto his scalp.

Capping the tube, I move around to study his face. Aside from the red flush over his cheekbones, his skin seems leached of color, with a gray undertone beneath his tan.

"No offense," I tell him, "but you look like shit."

Reed blinks slowly, as if his attention wasn't all there until I spoke to him. He focuses on me. "None taken, because I *feel* like shit."

"Worse or better than this morning?"

"The pain's better. Not great, but better. Overall, I'm just…tired."

"What about pukey?"

"Not anymore."

"That's good, at least. I can't be sure, because I don't have a thermometer, but I think you've got a fever."

"A fever," he echoes with a short laugh. "So I *haven't* been blushing all morning." When I don't respond to that, since I hadn't noticed any blushing in the first place, he eventually adds, "Thank you for lunch."

"You're welcome." I snag the ibuprofen off the counter and return to my seat. "These should help with the fever— and it's time for another dose. Then maybe go back to bed."

He nods without argument. "What are your plans for the rest of the day?"

I bite back my knee-jerk 'none of your fucking business.' If he can thank me, then I can also mind my manners. Besides, he's too sick to fight back. I might be vicious, but I'm not going to pick on someone weaker than I am.

And I suspect that he only asked because he's reluctant to stand up again. Delaying, because either his head or his leg hurts and he doesn't want to move yet.

I suppose I can help him delay. And what *am* I going to do? Dishes, first. After that? No idea. The tree decorations are finished but I can't go outside for a tree yet. I'd planned to fill most of my free time working on a new thrift-store canvas, but I won't paint while Reed Knowles is here. Even if he's sleeping. I just...don't want to open myself to anything he has to say. In general, I can take a lot of shit and my skin is fairly thick, but my art is one of my vulnerable points. I'm not going to put it on display where he can poke at it.

That leaves one option to fill the time. "I'll read, probably."

His eyes, which seemed a little glazed, sharpen with

pointed interest. He indicates Harris's small collection with a tilt of his head.

"One of those books over there?"

I shake my head. "I have some downloaded to my phone."

He appears disappointed by that answer. Then a strange expression rolls over his features. Almost like embarrassment but not quite. "Good choice."

I don't know if he means reading is a good choice or if *not* reading one of Harris's books is a good choice (which I'd already decided, because even if my tastes ran in that direction, horror is a bit too on the nose in an isolated cabin). But the way Reed's eyelids droop, as if he's about to lose consciousness right there, makes all thought of reading material fly out of my head.

"Reed," I say and am relieved when he immediately meets my eyes. "Seriously. You do *not* look good. You should get into bed before that fever gets worse."

"I know it." He rubs his forehead. "But I'm going to take a shower first. See if some cold water helps cool me down."

A cold shower seems crazy to me—but to each their own, I guess. "Don't wash your hair. You'll just wash out the antibiotic cream."

"Good call. I wouldn't have thought of that until I was already doing it."

"And leave the door unlocked." When his brows lift, I explain, "In case you pass out."

He doesn't even pretend that's not a possibility. "If you hear a big thump, I'd appreciate a rescue."

"Not sure if I'll be able to rescue you, but I can at least turn off the water. I should warn you, though: if you see Hot Biscuit Slim about to use the litter in there, do whatever you must to save yourself. I'm not braving that. Just try not to breathe for about ten minutes."

He lifts a brow and glances over at my cat. Hot Biscuit Slim has usurped the seat of his armchair, sitting up with a lower leg extended like an exotic dancer's while he licks his belly. "It's that bad?"

"Not most of the time, not since I switched him over to grain free. But every once in a while he'll sneak food he's not supposed to eat and the stench reaches catastrophic levels. Unfortunately, that includes yesterday and the day before. I'm not sure if his system is cleared out yet. But it's seriously toxic."

"Yet you survived."

"Only because I've built up some immunity. The first week after I adopted him, I was unconscious more often than not. So I'm not sure what horrors would happen to you if you're ever locked in a tiny bathroom with him."

His lips twitch. "Consider me sufficiently warned."

ABOUT TWENTY MINUTES LATER, I wish that someone had sufficiently warned *me*. Not about Hot Biscuit Slim, but about what my poor little eyes would witness when Reed emerges from the bathroom wearing nothing but a towel around his hips.

I wasn't sure the small water heater could supply the

bathroom and the kitchen at the same time, so I haven't started on the dishes yet. Instead I'm still seated at the table, scrolling through the library on my phone, when the bathroom door opens—and there he is.

Half naked. And built like a lumberjack, for fuck's sake.

The thermal base layers he'd worn earlier hugged his body like a second skin, so I knew what he was working with. Every bit of Reed Knowles is solid. Thick. Not as ridiculously defined as a dehydrated superhero but not soft, either.

Yet if I'd been asked whether I'd pictured anything beneath those thermal layers—I hadn't, because it was Reed Knowles—but if I'd been asked, I'd have said he probably looks like a Ken doll underneath. Smooth and shiny and fake.

Ha ha. Yeah, no.

He's hairy.

And not in the way he *should* be hairy, with a carpet on his back and sprouting from the tops of his toes, with a sparse scraggle poking out around his nipples. Life just isn't that fair. Because he's the good kind of hairy—the kind that seems to emphasize the breadth of his chest and the strength of his legs, and *of course* he's got one of those yummy lines arrowing down the center of abdomen.

Maybe I should have known. Especially since he's sporting heavy stubble on his jaw that wasn't there last night. I should have realized he wasn't smooth and shiny. But I didn't think about it. So I'm not prepared for how lust grabs hold of my innards at the mere sight of him.

A few breathless, *horrible* moments of unbridled lust.

It doesn't last, because he begins a halting progress toward the bed. I might be vicious, but seeing someone so obviously in pain inspires the opposite of a panty drenching.

"Did the shower help?"

"A little." Reed reaches the bed and eases down to sit on the edge. "I won't have clean clothes until I get my pack, so I washed what I was wearing and hung them over the towel rod to dry. Feel free to move them if you need to."

"I will."

He pulls back the covers on the bed. The muscles in his arm and shoulder flex and I lock my eyes on my phone, not at all interested in what's happening over on that side of the cabin. Nope. Not at all. I'm absolutely not aware of the creak of the bedframe as I pick a book at random. I'm absolutely not imagining *anything*.

Then I don't have to imagine, because he hisses in a sharp breath. Instinctively I look up to see what hurt him—his leg. He's swinging his injured leg up onto the bed. His towel is hanging on the bedpost. And I get an eyeful of cock. A *large* eyeful. Even though it's flaccid…and following a cold shower.

I drag my gaze away. But I can still see it.

God help me.

I *am* inoculated against good looks. I'm not so immune to a male body that's tall and strong and thick (and good hairy), especially if all of his appendages are in tall and strong and thick proportion to the rest of him.

Reed Knowles has no place in the best Christmas ever. What's between his thighs, however, might be the perfect gift for anyone interested in getting their stocking stuffed.

I'm not. Despite the tightening under my belly. Despite the liquid warmth pooling down low. Despite the way my imagination just went into overdrive.

I'm not lusting after *him*. I'm lusting after that dick. That's totally normal. After all, it's been a while since I've gotten any that didn't run on batteries.

It's also not a state that will change anytime soon. Not with him. So I won't think about his overlarge appendage anymore. I'm just going to focus on my book.

And I *do* focus. I stare at the first page for a long time. But I don't read a single word.

NIGHT FALLS. A FEW MORE hours pass. I make dinner. Reed hasn't moved.

Leaden dread fills my stomach. Is he sicker than I realized? He hasn't shifted around on the bed. Not once.

Is he dead?

I should never have a baby. I don't even *like* Reed, but I'm still tiptoeing over to check whether he's breathing. A kid that I loved would never get any sleep with me hovering over them.

My heart thudding, I lean over his mouth and listen. *There.* A breath. Then another.

He's not dead.

My relief is short-lived when I place my hand on his

forehead. Even without a thermometer, there's no doubt. His fever is *much* worse.

Shit. I rush across the cabin, grab the ibuprofen and fill a glass of water.

"Reed!" I urgently whisper-hiss his name, then realize I don't need to be quiet. The point is to wake him up. "Reed!"

He mumbles and turns his head.

"Reed! You're burning up! Sit up for a minute."

His eyes open and he manages a disoriented, "Huh?"

"Come on, sit up. Your fever is worse, so you need to take this medicine."

His eyelids squeeze shut. "Head hurts."

"The medicine will help that, too. Come now, let's get you up."

It takes another minute to elevate him high enough to take the pills and water. I help his shaking hand support the glass through a few swallows.

He's still completely out of it when we're done. He looks around the cabin, blinking in confusion.

"Harris?"

"He's not here."

He focuses his bleary gaze on me. "Abbie."

"That's me." I still can't believe he remembered my name.

"You're not pretty."

Oh fuck. That cuts deep. It shouldn't. I don't care what this asshole thinks of me. But it still hurts and I jerk back from the bed as if stabbed.

"Vibrant." He lies back onto his pillow and a blissful

expression comes over his face as he regards me. "That's the word I was looking for. Not pretty. You're *vibrant*. Like a fire. Burning warm and bright. Alive. A-lively." His brow furrows. "Lovely. Beautiful."

Usually when I'm blindsided, I laugh and joke to cover any nervousness or disbelief. But Reed knocks me so far past 'surprised' that I flip all the way back around to serious.

"You must be *really* sick." It's the only explanation for what he just said.

"I'm hot." A plaintive note enters his voice, and I suddenly have an image of him as a three year old. He begins pushing off the blankets.

Before he reveals more than his bare stomach, I grab half the covers and pull them back up. "I know you're hot, but the cabin will get very cold soon." My god, I'm even talking to him like he's a three year old. "So at least keep the sheet and this blanket on. And I've got a wet washcloth here, see? It's nice and cool. We'll put it on your forehead. How does that feel?"

His eyes close. "Feels better."

"Good." *You big man-baby.* "Do you want anything to eat before you go back to sleep?"

"Just you. I'd eat you up." A little smile curls his lips. "I bet you'd be sweet."

Blindsided again. "Sweet? Have you *met* me?"

"You're taking care of me. That's sweet."

"That doesn't mean *I* would be," I say dryly. "I'm far more tart than sweet."

61

"Piquant, then. All over my tongue."

He's wearing a blissful expression again, with his eyes closed and that little smile curving his mouth. His breath evens out. Already asleep—while my heart is thundering away. I stare at him, a million naughty thoughts racing through my head.

The naughtiest and worst of them all: *Maybe he's not so bad.*

I whirl away from the bed. Am I really trying to make myself believe Reed Knowles is a better person just because he said I was vibrant? And beautiful? And because I *think* he suggested that he'd enjoy eating me out, though it's far more likely that he has cannibalistic tendencies?

I'm not that naïve. Or that susceptible to flattery. I'm not.

It's just…it *is* pleasant to hear a kind word now and then. Though I'd rather hear those compliments from someone I care about, not from a mortal enemy. Maybe I'm trying to make him into a better person so that his words matter more. So I can take them to heart and believe them.

But I know better than that. Every shitty boyfriend I've ever had knew how to say nice things, and the ones who cheated were especially good at it. Hell, even my mother knows how to say nice things. But her compliments always come with an agenda attached, so the real trick is figuring out what she wants.

What *I* want is for those kind words to be *genuine.* Though I suppose Reed spoke the truth, because he seemed too disoriented to manipulate or lie. That doesn't make him a good guy.

And I don't need to make him into one.

As for the rest of those naughty thoughts, they truly don't matter. Nothing will come of them. Because when a Knowles and a Walker get together, the only outcome is death and disaster. I don't need that in my life.

Reed wouldn't want it, either. No question of that. Sure, in a feverish delirium, he confessed to finding me physically attractive. So what? I think he's physically attractive, too. Not that I would ever admit it. If I was sick or drunk, though, could it slip out? Sure.

But I won't take any attraction seriously. And I won't think about it anymore. Because he's Reed Knowles. Gorgeous on the outside, hideous on the inside. Not to mention, experiencing a jolt of animal lust isn't the same as wanting someone.

And I could never—absolutely never ever *ever*—want him.

BY THE TIME I'VE SHOWERED, dried and braided my hair in front of the fire, and prepared for bed, Reed's temperature seems to be lower. Though he pushed them off earlier, I tuck the comforter and quilt up around his shoulders—I know he's feverish, but it truly freezes in here when the fire is low, and I suspect exposure to the cold would be worse for him than the extra warmth.

That done, I carefully crawl over his sleeping form and onto my side of the bed. It's already toasty warm between the sheets. The first night, without him, I lay shivering under the covers until my body heat warmed everything up.

So I guess Reed being here isn't *all* bad. Just mostly bad.

Ugh. And I can't settle. I can't even blame Reed, because I didn't have the same trouble last night after he'd come stumbling in out of the storm. I simply ignored his presence until I fell asleep. When I gave him any thought, it was to hope he wouldn't die. I had no awareness of him as an attractive man who was sharing my bed.

I'm aware now, though. Disturbingly conscious of how he's right beside me, big and hairy and naked.

My heart nearly stops when he murmurs in his sleep and turns onto his side, facing the middle of the bed. Almost touching me.

What will I do if he *does* touch me? What if, while gripped by another feverish delirium, he says I'm pretty— No, not pretty. Vibrant. Alive. Lovely. And while out of his mind, what if he reaches for me? Tries to kiss me? Rolls on top of me, pushing between my thighs, his big stiffened cock seeking a way inside? Would I shove him off the bed? Slap him awake?

Let him?

That thought shames me enough to break out of the fantasy. Of course I wouldn't let him. Not while he's in a delirious state. It would be the same as taking advantage of someone who's intoxicated.

"Abbie?" he mumbles softly.

I can hardly breathe. "Yes?"

No answer. Asleep again.

I lie on my back, listening to the quiet crackle of the

fire. Watching the dancing light and shadows on the ceiling. Clenching my thighs tight, so tight, because everything inside is aching.

I *really* wish Reed hadn't said I was beautiful.

So it's kind of his fault that I turn toward the wall, putting as much space between us as I can before slipping my hand into my panties. I slide two fingers over my clit—god, I'm already so slick. Closing my eyes, I try to picture *anyone* except Reed. But my mind doesn't obey and within seconds he's got my knees shoved wide and his cock sinking deep, deep, that heavy, thick body pushing me down into the mattress, his hands hard and grasping my hips, using his full strength to power each devastating thrust. Until I can't take any more, can't take it, and I—

I come with my teeth digging into my pillow. Silently, so silently. My entire body shaking. Praying I don't wake him.

He doesn't stir.

When my breathing returns to normal, I roll onto my back again, marveling over what I just did. That was the fastest I've *ever* come. And I did it while fantasizing about being fucked by the man who bulldozed my mother's house.

I might be a terrible person.

But I'm also blissfully relaxed now, and wonderfully sleepy. So I'll worry about how terrible I am in the morning.

Reed

I WAKE UP WITH A WARM, PURRING BALL SNUGGLED AGAINST my back.

Hot Biscuit Slim.

Of more concern is the soft body snuggled against my front. She's *not* purring. Since she's not snarling and biting, though, she must be asleep.

I wonder if I'm asleep, too. Dreaming. But, no. No fog today. My head's aching, but not like it was. My brain seems to be working again. Yet my memories go hazy when I try to remember anything after my shower yesterday. Vaguely I recall Abbie telling me to sit up. Saying that my fever's worse.

So she had to take care of me. Again.

That doesn't explain why we're suddenly cuddle buddies. So most likely, we rolled toward each other. I'm a side sleeper and I'm lying like I always do, with one arm wedged under my pillow. My other arm's caught somewhere between a blanket and a quilt. She's almost completely hidden under the covers, with the top of her head tucked under my chin. Something's nestled against my stomach—I'm guessing her hands. Her soft, slow breaths warm my neck.

And the brain fog must not be completely gone, because I've got a powerful urge to wrap her in my arms and haul her in tight. It takes everything I've got to fight it. This is Abbie *Walker*. I should be shoving her back onto her own side of the bed.

Though, she *is* on her side. We're both in the middle, but each on our own sides. Our enemy lines have been clearly marked for almost twenty years, however. So there *should* be a gap. Some kind of No Man's Land.

Now that I'm awake, I ought to move. She wouldn't like being so close to me. I *shouldn't* like it.

But she took care of me. That's softened me a bit. I figured compassion was an alien concept to all the Walker women.

I guess I'm wrong about that. Maybe I'm also wrong about some other shit.

So I'll try harder not to antagonize her. If she lets me. She's prickly as hell. And there's a strange ache in my chest, knowing she hates me. That ache wasn't there before.

Another, lower ache wasn't there before, either. Morning wood, I tell myself.

It's not. I didn't wake up hard. My cock's only rising because I can feel her against me. Because I can smell the sweet scent of her hair. Holding my breath only works for a minute. This is stupid. I should just move away from her.

Should just get out of this bed.

Nothing on this earth could make me.

And that's *before* Abbie nuzzles her face into my throat. Before her arm curls around my waist. Before her thigh slides over my hip.

A few realizations hit me all at once. First, I'm stark naked. Second, though she's wearing a flannel top, her legs are covered in nothing but bare, smooth skin. Third, the way she's pressed closer means the only barrier between my cock and her pussy is her underwear, and I can feel how soft and hot she is through that thin layer of fabric.

So soft and hot.

Fuck. I know what'll happen if she wakes up now. She'll think I was letting her do this on purpose to humiliate her. Not because the heat from her cunt is frying my brain. I've got to extricate myself from this. Even though I don't want to. I need to ease my way out of this bed without waking her up.

My every good intention is blasted apart when her hips begin to move. Rubbing that hot cunt up and down my shaft. I stifle a groan behind clenched teeth. I need to stop this. But the full force of my will is focused on *not* rolling Abbie onto her back and sinking balls deep.

A few more rubs, and the slight friction of cotton against my bare cock all but disappears. She's wet. Soaked-through-her-panties wet. Christ. I'm not going to come like this. Not. But I'm a fucking liar, I can already feel it, the deepening ache, the liquid blaze. I fight the sensation but can't muffle the tortured groan that pushes its way from my chest.

"Whuh?" It's a sleepy enquiry against my neck. Then she sucks in a horrified breath. "Ohmygod."

"Abb—"

Her head jerks up, whacks me under my chin. Stars explode behind my eyes. She pulls away from me so fast that she bounces against the wall on her side of the bed. "I'm sorry! I'm so sorry! I didn't— Fuck fuck fuck!"

She bounces back and over me. Hot Biscuit Slim yowls and streaks off the bed. Abbie nearly trips over him then rights herself again. By the time I sit up, she's across the cabin.

The bathroom door slams.

Fuck.

I stare into the dark until I feel the bite of cold air on my overheated skin. The blankets were thrown halfway to the foot of the bed during Abbie's flight. I could drag them up over me again, go back to sleep and forget all this.

I won't ever.

Better to get up and face her. Clothes are an issue, though. Mine are hanging up in the bathroom—and likely still wet. I can't get in there now, anyway.

But my brain's clearer than it was yesterday, so it occurs to me that Harris always has extra gear and clothing stored. We're almost the same size.

There's no fucking way I could have eased out of bed earlier like I'd planned. My leg's not as stiff but hurts so goddamn much that I still lurch and huff just to stand up. At least the freezing air takes care of my erection.

I strike gold in a bottom dresser drawer. Sweatpants and a thermal shirt that's a smidge too tight, but Harris won't care if I stretch out the cuffs. There's nothing to put on my feet, but the wool socks in my snow boots are dry and thick.

The fire's next. I toss wood onto the embers. It's still fucking freezing. I haul a quilted throw off the back of the armchair and wrap it around my shoulders. The same way I remember seeing Abbie do yesterday.

Nothing from the bathroom yet. She's got to be cold in there. She's wearing nothing on her legs or feet.

Hot Biscuit Slim sits by a little silver dish and glowers at me.

"Sorry, bud."

Abbie said something about a special diet, so I won't make the mistake of feeding him anything. I search for the coffee, instead.

I'm filling up the moka pot when Abbie appears again. She doesn't look my way. Just quickly pulls on her pajama pants and thick socks. Over it all goes her fuzzy robe.

Without a word, and still not looking at me, she crosses over to the cat's dish, fills it.

So it'll be up to me to break this silence. "Coffee's on."

"Thank you." Now she turns in my direction but doesn't meet my eyes. She gestures vaguely toward the bed. "If you can just forget—"

"It's forgotten." I'm lying. "You rolled in your sleep, I rolled in my sleep, and there's not much room in that bed. It wasn't intended, yeah?"

Her sheer disbelief in response to that question seems to blast away any lingering embarrassment. "Of course not. I'd rather cut off my arm."

Ouch. If I suffered from an overinflated ego, one conversation with Abbie Walker would cure me of it. "Then it's a good thing we were just mindlessly rolling around all night. A bloody stump of an arm might ruin your perfect Christmas."

She stares at me, her lips compressed. I suspect she's trying hard not to laugh.

So there's my new purpose in life. I intend to make Abbie Walker laugh. Though that might be too ambitious, considering how long she's despised me. Maybe just a smile.

But I'll settle for her wet pussy all over me again.

And I need to hold that thought, because these sweats don't hide a damn thing. But when I turn back toward the stove, it's my limp that catches her attention.

"Did I hurt your leg worse? When I—"

"You never even touched it." I cut her off, not liking the guilt shadowing her eyes. "It's actually better. Still hurts like hell and I wouldn't want to poke it, but it's overall better. Now, what are your thoughts about breakfast? You cooked for me yesterday, I'll cook today. But it's your food."

"I usually eat later. Coffee first. Then toast or an orange." Her brow furrows. "But you must be starving. You barely ate yesterday."

"I could do with something." That's an understatement.

"Then most of the breakfast stuff is here." She brushes

past me to open a cupboard, bringing with her that sweet scent again. Maybe from her shampoo. She's bound her glorious mass of hair into two braids, as if she washed it just before bed. "Potatoes are over there. Eggs and bacon in the fridge. Sausage in the freezer."

I'm still looking through the cupboard and concealing my body's reaction to her scent and her nearness and those braids. "You weren't kidding about having enough food for the both of us. You stocked up."

"My vacation is for two weeks. But Harris said I might be snowed in for even longer, so I brought extra. And since this holiday was a chance to cook what I actually like to eat, I loaded up on stuff I wanted. Or might want. Hence the breakfast stuff, even though I usually don't eat much for breakfast."

My attention snags on one part of that. "You usually don't cook what you like?"

Her expression goes stony. For a second I think she won't answer. Then she says stiffly, "I mean that I only had my own preferences to consider."

"Lucky for me, then. Because judging by this cupboard, we have similar preferences."

She scowls. Apparently not thrilled by the thought of us having anything in common.

The gurgling of the coffee pot saves her from having to reply—or saves me from her reply. She takes her mug to sit in front of the fire.

Feeling as if this whole morning has been like getting

struck by a lightning bolt—or maybe just another tree branch—I spend a few seconds staring into the cupboard and trying to recover. Soon enough, though, my stomach reminds me that I'm starving.

I pull out the pancake mix and can barely focus on the directions. That's not Abbie, distracting me. My brain aches while trying to make out the blurry words.

Fuck. This is the last thing I need. But I suppose as hard as I whacked my head, it might be a few more days—hopefully not weeks—before I can read without my brain disintegrating.

"Abbie?"

She glances away from the fire, eyebrow raised.

"Is this one of the 'just add water' mixes?" When her forehead furrows, I explain, "I apparently can't focus on small type yet."

Her lips part in realization. "Oh. Yeah, it is. Do you need me to measure out the—"

"I've got it," I say when she begins to get up from her chair. "I know what the consistency should be. I just wasn't sure if water was all it needed."

"Just water," she confirms.

While the griddle is heating, I glance over at Abbie again. Now there's a sight that doesn't make my head ache. She's got her phone off the battery charger and is curled up in the armchair. Every little while, she swipes the screen with her thumb. Turning a page.

That's irresistible to me. "What book did you choose?"

She gives me a long, narrow look. As if thinking about not answering. Then, "*Otherlands*."

The title sounds familiar but I can't place it. "Is it science fiction?"

"Science, but not fiction." She scoots around in the chair so that she's facing me a little better. "It's by a paleontologist who goes backward through time with each chapter, explaining how different animals flourished or went extinct when their environments changed."

Ah, that's where I've heard of it. "I have that. Haven't read it yet. But you're enjoying it? It's interesting?"

"*So* interesting. Like, did you know that grass was barely even a thing when dinosaurs were alive? I always pictured them resembling herds of buffalo, grazing on the grassy plains. Or with the tall ones eating trees while the short ones ate grass. But grass only became dominant after the dinosaurs were gone."

Vibrant. When did I decide that was how to describe her? Yet it's the perfect word for her. "I didn't know. I always pictured them the same way."

"I also didn't know the Mediterranean was empty at one point. The whole sea was nothing but a giant basin full of salt because it was cut off from the Atlantic at the Strait of Gibraltar and dried up. But when the strait opened, there was catastrophic flooding and massive waterfalls as it filled again."

I knew that one. But I don't want to seem like I'm trying to one-up her. I won't pull that kind of shit, but she doesn't know that about me yet. "You like prehistoric stuff, then?"

"I do," she says—warily, as if waiting for me to trash her.

I'd be the last person to do that. "You might like that third book over there." I gesture to Harris's collection. "It includes zombie megafauna that were trapped in ice until the glaciers melt."

Amusement brightens her expression. "Really?"

"Really."

"I'm almost tempted. I don't read much fiction. But maybe I'll give it a try if my battery pack runs out of juice. Because I planned to recharge it in the car, but I don't want to shovel out three feet of snow just to open the car door."

At least three feet. But the snow seems to be tapering off. "You have chains on your tires?"

"I do."

Leaving here is probably at least a week away, but I ought to give us both something to look forward to. "Once the roads are clear enough, will you drive me to where I left my truck? It's not far. Just a few miles to the cutoff road, then up another driveway. You can drop me off and get back to your vacation."

"I will. Gladly." Her arch look takes the bite out of that response.

"Are you still planning to find a tree once it stops snowing?"

"I am."

"If you give me another day to rest up this leg, I'll help."

By the dismay on her face, she's looking for a polite way to tell me to fuck off. She goes with, "I don't need help."

"But *I* might. I have to get my pack. And with this bump on my head, it'd be smarter to have someone out there with me."

"Oh. All right, then."

Again, willing to help me. Though it's clear that, otherwise, she'd rather have nothing to do with me. Yet she does anyway.

A faint memory floats through my head. Maybe it was a dream. Telling Abbie that she was beautiful. And so sweet for taking care of me.

But I've heard that before, haven't I? Harris knows there's history between the Walkers and the Knowles, so he doesn't talk about her much. Not to me. But when he does say anything, it's always something good. Which is no small thing, coming from Harris.

I turn back to the griddle, trying hard to remember what I had against Abbie, specifically. That shit with our parents running off together...that's old news. My dad let it rule his life. Same with her mom. But it's stupid to hold a grudge against another kid for what our cheating parents did almost twenty years ago.

She *did* bite me. Fuck me if I can recall what started it, though. What provoked her? Maybe I did or said something—or she simply went crazy with grief.

Hell, maybe it was just the inevitable result of the toxic shit our parents were throwing at each other, because that was impossible to escape. Abbie couldn't have been, what—six years old? Seven? Likely she doesn't even remember the incident. I only remember because I held onto it, resenting her for attacking me at my mom's funeral, of all places. But my dad held onto it tighter. Continually reminding me of what she'd done. Feeding that resentment. He was the one who first called her vicious. A description that was reinforced every time I saw the scar. *The vicious one did that to me.*

She never did anything else. Resenting her simply became a habit.

Her sister and her mother, though…they earned more of that resentment. But even the sister, hell—the last time anything came up was in high school. I avoided her, but now and then had to defend myself against suggestions that I was cheating on my tests, or screwing around on my girlfriends, or bringing in weed to sell. And there was no doubt in my mind who started that shit, every time. Because that's always the Walker refrain: the Knowles family has no morals or ethics and we'll fuck over anyone for a dime.

Even if the sister started those rumors, however, it wouldn't surprise me to learn her mother prodded her into it. Angela Walker has never stopped waging her campaign against everything my family has ever touched. That woman, she's a real piece of work.

But my dad is, too. So I can feel some sympathy for both those girls, growing up around that shit. Especially for Abbie, now that I've seen more of who she is.

What it all boils down to, though, is that I've assumed she'd be like her sister and mother, but I don't actually know much about Abbie herself. Except paleontology makes her eyes light up. And she'll take care of someone even if she hates them.

Maybe I can work on that hating part. Because her feelings toward me are likely based on the same old grudges and the assumption that I'm just like my father.

I'm not.

Hopefully I'll get started on improving her opinion by pulling my own weight—and filling her stomach. "I've got pancakes ready if you want some."

She seems torn. It's not easy to accept anything from me. I get it. I had the same inner debate while she was keeping me upright the other night.

Finally she nods and uncurls from her chair. "Thanks."

The tension underlying the quiet in the cabin seems to ease, as if that single word forms a truce between us. An uneasy truce, but a truce nonetheless. I lay out the plates and silverware. She grabs real maple syrup from the cupboard, followed by peanut butter.

Again, the same preferences. "Crunchy peanut butter. You're a woman after my heart."

"Maybe." Pointedly she picks up a table knife.

I grin and refill her coffee, then notice Hot Biscuit Slim at my feet, gazing up at us pitifully. "I'm guessing he can't have pancakes."

"Not unless he makes them himself."

As she says it, a not-quite-a-smile tugs at her mouth. There's a joke there I'm not getting. Probably something about his name. I still can't remember where it's from. But

I put it away for later.

I'm too hungry to talk much. She's quiet, too, though she's not shoveling it in like I am. Instead she's neat about it. I whack off a wedge of pancake with the tines of my fork, while she cuts little triangular bites with her table knife. It's fascinating to watch. I can almost hear the admonishment behind that kind of eating. Back in the day, my grandmother would have rapped my knuckles if I didn't mind my manners and cut my food the same way, but those lessons didn't stick past childhood. Watching Abbie, I'd bet anything her mother drilled that into her from a very young age...and never let up.

But what's really fucking wild is that this dainty eater once took a bite of my hand. And would have brained me with a poker if I'd made one wrong move that first night.

I'm guessing she's got a polite, serene layer that was developed over a long time, and that's what most people see. I haven't seen much of it. Instead, I've seen the fire that burns through that polite layer.

If true, I'm not sorry that she hasn't been polite and serene. I like the fire.

When the chasm in my stomach has a heap of pancakes at the bottom, I slow down and search for something that'll help me get to know her—and for her to know me. I have to tread carefully. We have one point in common for sure. Well, two points. But no way in fuck will I bring up my mom and her dad running off and dying together. So we have one point in common that's a viable direction.

"You've been working for Harris how long?"

"Four years." That seems like it'll be it. Then she apparently decides to make an effort, too. Those good manners kicking in. "You've been friends since high school?"

"Elementary. He lived just a block over from us." And this is already veering too damn close to the point I won't mention—how Harris was there after my mom died. How I was always over at his place to avoid my dad. Abbie seems to recognize the danger, too. She's cutting a triangle smaller and smaller. "Is he a good boss?"

"He is. Not always easy to work for but...generous." She casts her gaze around the cabin, as if to indicate that her trip here was part of that generosity.

Which is exactly like Harris. Yet for a moment, something heavy and dark grips my chest. Wondering if there's something more between them. Wondering if his generosity might have another meaning than the obvious.

But if Harris was interested in Abbie Walker, he'd be out here with her. He wouldn't have left her to face an intruder with only a poker.

"He is generous," I agree finally. Reeling a bit. Was that *jealousy* that just hit me?

It couldn't be.

At least now the cabin is another point in common that's safe to discuss. She asks, "Do you come out here often with him?"

"By myself, usually—when I'm on deadline or I don't want any distractions. It's a good place to be alone with only your own thoughts for company."

"I thought it would be, too," she says dryly. Then, "On deadline?"

Before I can stop myself, my gaze shoots to the paperbacks under the side table.

Shit. I'd been so thrown off by the jealousy gripping my chest, I didn't even think about what came out of my mouth. My books aren't something I tell people about. Particularly since my earliest work hits real close to home. Anyone who knows me would recognize the basis for a whole slew of characters.

Including the Walkers.

I look away quick, but Abbie's not slow. Her eyebrows shoot sky high.

"Do you come out here to sneakily read or to sneakily write about zombie megafauna?"

"Write." No point in lying.

"And that's why you came out here this time?"

I nod, though it's only partially true. Until the shitshow at my dad's lodge, I had no intention of visiting the cabin. But once I left, my plan was to come here and write. I cleared a few weeks off my schedule to plow through a first draft, but the beginning of the story is giving me more trouble than I've ever had. And now I've lost a couple of days when I could have been working, thanks to the concussion. I'll have to make up for it.

Her eyebrows draw down in a puzzled frown. "You're an author, then—but I thought you were an engineer?

Something like that?"

"A structural engineer. I do house inspections."

I don't consider it an unusual profession but her confusion deepens. "Inspections? What kind?"

"For people buying or selling their houses. Usually for people buying, making sure there aren't any hidden issues that will cost a fortune to fix down the road."

"Oh." The reason for her confusion becomes clear when she adds, "I always assumed you worked with your dad."

I can't stop my short, bitter laugh. "No. I'm an independent contractor."

"Ah." Her gaze falls to her plate, where her fingers are clenched tightly around her knife and fork. "So you don't work for him. But you were there when he bulldozed my mom's house."

"That reason was more personal." And ended up being a day that opened my eyes to who my father truly was.

No, that's not right. My eyes had been opened for a while. But it was one of the final nails in the coffin of our relationship. Not *the* final nail. That happened right before I came here.

And we've gone way outside of our safe zone. I try to steer us back.

"So, what exactly is it you do for Harris?"

At some point I hope to make her smile, but the one she offers now is a twisted, sneering version of one. "I throw shit in his face, then say it's his own damn fault. Then I never take responsibility for the damage I do."

A syrupy glob of pancake and peanut butter wedges itself in my gullet. For a second, I think that must have been something my dad said. But, no. It was me. Harris told me that he was hiring a Walker girl, and I shot back with a variation of the same thing I'd likely said a dozen times to him over the years.

Harris must have told Abbie. Knowing him, he thought she'd get a laugh.

She's not laughing. Abruptly she stands and carries her plate to the sink.

I never take responsibility for the damage I do. I said that about her. But the description fits me, instead. Saying shit that could have cost her a job. A good job. Though I didn't really know a thing about her.

I need to apologize, but the pancake is still stuck in my throat. Then she returns to her armchair by the fire but turns her back toward me. Clearly not wanting to hear anything I might possibly have to say.

I *will* apologize. When she's ready to listen. I don't think she'd listen right now.

And I hope to fuck she never reads my first book.

Abbie

THOUGH REED SAID HE WAS FEELING BETTER, THE MORN-ing's activity apparently saps his energy. By ten, he's in bed again. Either a belly full of pancakes put him to sleep, or the lingering effects of his concussion did.

Maybe both.

When I hear him moving around late in the afternoon, I nix any further attempt at conversation by putting in earbuds and pretending he doesn't exist. That works until I have to sit at the same table again.

Dinner is pappardelle with a meaty tomato sauce, sautéed veggies, and garlic bread. The last guy I dated would have been whining about carbs at this point. Not that he lasted. It only took my sister and my mother moving in to run him off.

Mom would have also complained about the carbs, despite no one forcing her to fill her plate with more pasta than vegetables. And she'd have lamented that if she skips the bread, it will go to waste (though if I'd skipped making a serving for her in anticipation of her *not* wanting the carbs, she would have complained that I didn't make enough for everyone or that I'm implying she's fat and pushing her to diet.) Lauryn would have looked at the pasta box and declared that she'd have chosen a different brand or that we should always make our own pasta (not that she would help)—and then, if I *do* make the pasta myself, demand that I use free-range eggs (I already do, but she checks the carton each time to make sure) and a non-GMO artisan flour that she heard about online (though she doesn't buy it herself or offer to pay the difference.)

Reed's not complaining about carbs, though. He's not complaining about anything. He genuinely seems to enjoy the meals I've made so far…which is a novelty.

I feel his gaze on my face while we eat, but I'm still using my earbud protection. *At the table.* It's rude, beyond rude, I can barely even stand myself right now, but there's a weight in my chest growing heavier and heavier with every passing minute. I'm afraid if he says one word to me, just one—it doesn't even matter *what* he says—I'll burst into tears.

But it's not because of Reed. Not really. It's just…I only wanted one thing during this holiday. One simple thing. To spend a few days away from people who criticize and judge and who simply cannot fucking *leave me be.*

Though Reed *is* leaving me be. I recognize that. But I also wanted to spend time painting—and I'm too afraid of what he might say if I do. It's not even that I care about his opinion. I don't. But I don't want to open myself up to any criticism he might have. It's the same reason I'm not playing Christmas carols on the portable speaker like I did the first day. Yesterday, I wouldn't have anyway, while his head was clearly hurting. Or while he was sleeping. But I won't now, either. Having been around my mom and sister makes it impossible for me to sing out loud in front of anyone else. I don't have a great voice, I know it. It's scratchy and always off-key. But I *like* singing. It makes me happy. Yet I know from experience that it only takes one snide comment to make me feel like shit, instead.

I'm so tired of always having to protect myself. So I just wanted a few days where I didn't have to walk around with my armor on. I can't do that at home. I'd hoped I could here.

But Reed's here now. And even though he was so nice about me rubbing against him this morning, though he's been so nice about the food, though he said nice things in his delirium, I feel as if I'm waiting for the knife to come out. And why wouldn't it? He's always hated us. And he said plenty of shit before. Do I really think he would stop at tearing down a house when I'm right here to tear down, instead?

I don't.

So I just want to be alone. I just want to be alone. Where it's safe.

REED SILENTLY VOLUNTEERS TO DO the dishes by starting on

them after finishing his dinner. I let him have at it, change into my pajamas, and head to my armchair to read. I don't look up from my phone when he eventually joins me in front of the fireplace. His big frame fills the oversized chair, where he sits with his feet extended toward the flames and his eyes closed for almost two hours. Then he heads to bed.

Though I'm exhausted, I don't follow. Instead I toss another piece of wood onto the fire, return to the armchair, and arrange the quilted throw over as much of me as it will cover. I set my phone aside and close my eyes.

I don't know what time it is when I wake up shivering, my back aching. The fire's low. I need to add more wood. But before I uncurl my legs, a massive shadow blots out the light from the fireplace and I'm scooped up against Reed's broad chest.

He doesn't say a single word as he carries me to the bed. He doesn't have to. It was stupid to stay in the chair.

Though maybe he believes I'm asleep. Because I don't say anything, either. I should. What kind of arrogant asshole bodily grabs someone and relocates them? I should be telling him off. Instead, I drowsily wallow in his warmth and the strength of the arms holding me.

But I can't bear a repeat of the previous morning. Of waking to find myself writhing against his cock like a deranged Aladdin trying to rub a genie out of a lamp.

So as soon as he sets me on the bed, I shove myself all the way against the far wall. I'm still wearing my socks and pajama pants. If I hope to sleep, I need to take them off.

I don't. I'm too afraid of falling asleep. Too afraid of what I'll do. So I spend a miserable night, with my pants twisting around my legs every time I move and my socks irritating the fuck out of me and overheating my feet.

Reed sleeps restlessly, turning and turning. Or maybe he's also awake. A few heavy sighs come from that side of the bed. A couple of times, the quiet within the cabin seems *so* thick—as if he's about to say something.

He doesn't.

BY MORNING, MY EXHAUSTION HAS become a stupor, complete with a bonus headache. But I don't ignore Reed anymore. It just makes me feel shittier.

Maybe because it's Christmas Eve, we both make a concerted effort to be pleasant. Every word that passes our lips is careful. Polite. Safe. The weather has cleared, so we agree to go tree hunting after we eat—toast for me, eggs and toast for him. At the table, our conversation is courteous drivel.

"More coffee?"

"Yes, thank you. How are the eggs?"

"Perfect, thank you. I can never flip them without breaking the yolk."

"I'll show you the next time I make them."

"That'd be great, thank you. I'll do the dishes again when we get back with the tree."

"I appreciate that, thank you. For dinner, do you have any Christmas Eve tradition that you'd like to follow? Assuming we have the ingredients, of course."

"I don't, but thank you for asking. I'm happy to eat whatever you traditionally have."

"It's not a traditional thing for me. It's just something I wanted to do when I planned my menus. I thought to make finger foods—as a late lunch/early dinner—so that I can graze while decorating the tree."

"A finger food free-for-all sounds damn good. What are you thinking of including?"

"A charcuterie board with the usual things, plus veggies and spinach dip—and so it's not all cold stuff, sausage rolls and jalapeño poppers."

"Hell, yeah. What kind of sausage rolls?"

"They're those cocktail-sized ones that come frozen. They're easy to throw in the oven along with the poppers."

"I bet I'll eat about fifty of those."

That absurdity gets us through breakfast. Then Reed dons his snow suit and heads out to the shed for the sled, bow saw, and two pairs of snowshoes. I don't have fancy snow gear but I bundle up, then step out onto the porch to wait for him.

It's absolutely glorious outside. Azure skies. Majestic firs. Pristine snow.

For the first time in what seems like forever, the weight in my chest eases. The temperature's just below freezing but the sun on my face makes the air seem warmer, fresh and exhilarating instead of biting and bitter.

I close my eyes and just breathe it in.

The crunch of snow alerts me to Reed's return from

around the back of the cabin—the uneven rhythm of his steps telling me that, despite what he says, his leg must still be hurting him. Or maybe his injury is aggravated by the difficulty of walking in the snow.

Reed grins when he spots me on the porch. "Pretty nice day, yeah?"

"It is." His grin does fluttery little things to my insides, so I look away.

"You've got your tree permit?"

I pat my coat pocket.

"What are the restrictions?"

"No cutting within two hundred feet of a riverbank, lake, or a meadow. And it can't be over fifteen feet tall." A height which wouldn't even fit inside the cabin.

"No worries there, then." He drops the second pair of snowshoes by my feet. "Need help strapping these on?"

"I've got it."

It takes me a few minutes to get used to walking with them, but I'm doing all right by the time we leave the clearing and start down the road. Reed keeps pace beside me, dragging the sled.

All the Douglas firs around us are much taller than fifteen feet, but I don't care if it takes us a while to find one suitable for a Christmas tree. It's so beautiful out here. So quiet, too, even with the noise we're making. And I don't know if it's the fresh air, or simply being outside of the cabin for the first time in days, but my exhaustion and headache are gone. So is the dark and heavy mood that almost crushed me yesterday.

"This is the best smell," I find myself saying, and Reed glances at me, his brows raised. "Fresh snow."

"Yeah, it is." He watches as I bend to sweep up a handful of powder, smash it between my gloved palms, and hurl the clump at a tree. "Are you itching for a snowball fight?"

I sniff derisively. "Snowball fights are something you do with friends, not your sworn enemy."

"You'd prefer to fight with your friends than an enemy?"

"Of course. Friendly fights are the best."

"Are they?"

"They are. Because you know a friend won't hurt you on purpose. So instead of a fight, it becomes more of a battle of skill or wits. Or just pure fun."

"Fun? I should probably warn you of a battle I'm fighting, then. I"—he pauses until I turn my head to look at him—"am going to make you laugh. Or smile."

"Do you *like* losing? Is that why you're flinging yourself into a battle that you can't possibly win?"

He shrugs. "I've never lost a challenge before."

"Never?"

"Never. And I won't start today."

So arrogant. I roll my eyes. Then I plow ahead of him, because I *might* smile. I might. "How far is your snowmobile? I'm assuming you came by the road."

But there's no sign of the machine yet. I don't expect to see any tracks, but the snowmobile itself should be visible, even if it's covered by snow. The forest is mostly clear of underbrush between the trees and the ground is even, so a snowmobile-sized heap will stick out.

"I did come by the road. It can't be far."

It *is* far. At least a mile, which is a ridiculous distance in the snow. And even with the snowshoes, trudging through the powder takes its toll. By the time I spot the tree branch that must have whacked him, Reed's limp is more pronounced. I'm sweating, and my lungs and leg muscles burn.

"There." I point to a tree on the side of the road. Near its base is a snowy heap. Red and silver show through the white where the wind scoured the snow away.

While Reed begins digging out his pack, I look farther down the narrow lane. The limb that fell on him is still partially attached to the tree and hangs down into the road. It's no small branch. At least four or five inches thick where the limb cracked—and to break like that, the bough must have been additionally burdened with a substantial amount of snow.

And all that weight crashed down on him.

"You were *really* lucky," I tell him seriously. Not just surviving the impact but then finding his way through the blizzard to the cabin.

He's looking at the broken bough, too. Something in his face tells me that he hadn't realized how large it was or how far from the cabin he'd been. Then he glances at me. "It's worse than that." He gestures to the large hiking backpack now strapped to the sled. "My keys are in there."

I stare at him in disbelief. "So if I hadn't been at the

cabin…"

"Maybe I could have broken in, but the state I was in? Maybe not." He shakes his head—and seems to shake away all the morbid thoughts. "Anyway. Let's go get your tree."

I've caught my second wind, so I'm ready to. I'm not sure he is. "Are you doing all right? Your head, your leg?"

"I can keep going."

That *doesn't* answer how his head and leg are doing, and the evasion tells me they hurt like hell. "Do you want me to pull the sled?"

The look he gives me is an emphatic, *Not a fucking chance.*

So we keep heading down the road. I don't know why I thought there'd be little trees everywhere. But I suppose any tree shorter than three feet is covered in snow. Though there's a dearth of medium trees, too.

Now that we've got Reed's pack, though, we can search away from the road. "Harris said the best place to look is near the crag. Do you know where that is?"

"I do." His huff of laughter emerges on a frozen breath. "It's about a mile on the other side of the cabin."

Shit. Well, I'm not going to make him walk that far. Not for this. "Let's keep looking here, then."

"We can head to the crag, if you want."

"It's fine. Besides—" A Christmas miracle. "Look there. That one."

Reed frowns. "Which one?"

"That one. Right where I'm pointing."

He drags the sled closer to me, as if to make sure he's

got the same view through the trees. "That skinny one with only four branches?" he asks doubtfully.

"Yep."

"You're sure? We can head to the crag. No need to settle for that one. Unless you *want* a Charlie Brown tree."

My stomach knots. "If I wanted a perfect tree lot tree, I could have brought one."

"And if you're choosing this one because of my leg, it's fine. We can keep looking."

"I don't want to keep looking. I found my tree."

His eyes narrow. "And you're telling me *that* tree fits into your best Christmas ever? This is what you pictured?" My expression must show some of what I'm feeling because he holds up his hands, as if in surrender. "I'm just trying to make sure you get the Christmas you wanted."

"And I just pictured *a* tree. *Any* tree," I insist, and his blatant skepticism yanks at the knot of emotions inside me, pulling tighter and tighter and tighter...until it snaps. "My perfect Christmas is screwed anyway, isn't it? You're here. And you and your dad are the whole fucking reason I came out here in the first place!"

His face darkens. "What the hell are you talking about?"

"You bulldozed my mother's home!" I scream at him, throwing my hands wide. "After your father stole it out from under her. After she spent every bit of her savings fighting to keep it. So where did she and my sister go? To *my* house! And your dad's out there gloating over how she lost her home, how she lost everything. Have you seen how much it costs to rent? She can't find anything decent, especially now that her credit's fucked! So I have to hide in my own house because I can't even walk in the door without them criticizing every choice I've ever made. And I hate it!"

Blinded by tears, by fury, by hurt, I snatch up a fistful of snow and fling it at the blurry giant figure that is Reed Knowles. "I hate it! And I hate every Knowles man alive for going after us, and going after us, and tearing us down! Wasn't it enough to badmouth me to Harris?" I hurl another snowball. "You had to take their house? And now I can't do anything without them sniping and sniping and sniping—and when they aren't sniping about me, they're sniping about everything else in the world. So my perfect Christmas? It's not the fucking tree! It's just being away from them. Away f-from the c-constant—"

My voice breaks. Despair rushes in, heavy in my chest. So heavy. Crushing me.

"And I have to go back!" Covering my face, I sob into my hands. "Oh god, I have to go back."

"Don't. No. Abbie." Reed's voice is low, rough—and so close. Then he wraps me in his arms, brings me in against his chest and I can't even fight him. My fists clutch his coat and I hold on tight, sobbing into his shoulder.

Gradually I become aware of the soothing hum he's making, and his hand stroking up and down my back. And this is worse, a million times worse, than waking up while rubbing against his dick.

My face is likely swollen and pink. I'm an ugly crier. So

beet-red embarrassment won't make much difference.

Body stiffening, I pull away. I can't look at him as I mumble, "Sorry."

"Hey, no." Removing his gloves, he gently cups my face in his hands. "You took care of me. It's my turn to do the same for you."

He couldn't know how that statement would affect me. My gaze flies to his, and I see nothing but concern there. And warmth. Has *anyone* ever taken care of me? People have done what they think is best for me. But has anyone taken care of me in a way that I actually felt *cared* for, even for a few measly minutes? I can't think of one person.

Except for Reed Knowles. Of all people.

"Now you've got to let me apologize," he says, his thumbs wiping the tears from my cheeks. "First of all, I'm sorry for badmouthing you to Harris. I knew nothing about you. So I should have kept my mouth shut. I was wrong, it was a shitty thing to do, and you deserved better."

I don't trust my voice yet, so I just give a small nod. Accepting that apology.

He takes a deep breath. "And the second thing… Fuck, I'm sorry for this. I'm so sorry to tell you this. But your mom was the one who approached my dad about taking the house off her hands."

I jerk back, staring up into his face. "What?"

His eyes are solemn. "The assessed value of the house *did* increase and the property taxes went up—but most do over time, and there are state limits on the increase. Something like three percent a year. That wasn't the real issue, though."

"Not the real issue?" I shake my head. "I saw the bill. The amount she owed was ridiculous. It was impossible to pay."

"Because she hadn't paid in over fifteen years."

"*What?*" I wheeze the question as if I've been punched.

"From what I could tell, when the mortgage was paid off—which likely included the property tax payment—she ignored the new tax bills the county sent."

I close my eyes. Still reeling. But thinking back…I *did* see the huge amount owed. My mom showed me that. But never a statement with the breakdown. "So they held off for fifteen years?"

"Not quite. But whenever they started to threaten a levy, she'd go in and make promises. Make payment arrangements. She'd keep those up for a while then stop. And a levy never moves quick—not in our county, anyway. But after fifteen years, they began moving toward taking the house. It never actually went to auction, though. Is that what she said happened? That's why you thought my dad got it for nothing?"

"It is," I say, feeling utterly numb. "But she went to him?"

"Yeah. I *was* there for that. He called me up, said he had a gift for me. That meeting was when I saw the paperwork, the history. She said she didn't want the hassle of trying to sell it through a realtor. She just wanted it off her hands." He shakes his head. "But she shouldn't have an issue finding another place. His company paid cash, and after settling the outstanding taxes…that should have left her about four hundred K in the bank."

I stagger and trip over my snowshoes, dropping to the snow in a tangled heap. "Four hundred thousand?!"

His grim nod is like another punch to my gut. I can't take the hand he offers to help me up. I can only stare up at him while everything I thought I knew crashes down around me.

Four hundred thousand. While all this time, she hasn't been paying for much of anything—saying she's saving up for another place. But although it sucks that she hasn't been helping out financially while living in my house, it's not what rips into me the most.

What hurts are the lies. The guilt trips.

The majority of the money I used to buy my house was from my share of my father's life insurance and the trust he left for each of us. That's the weapon my mom pulls out whenever I gently suggest they start looking for their own place—because isn't it horrible and selfish to use money earned off my dad's death to buy a home, but not gladly welcome the rest of his family to live there, too?

Since I haven't taken Reed's hand, have just sat in the snow staring up at him stupidly, he crouches beside me— with clenched teeth and a hiss, as if the movement pulls painfully at his leg. Yet he focuses his concern on me.

"Are you all right?"

"No." My voice wavers as if I might burst into tears again. Whatever happened to not allowing Reed Knowles to see any of my vulnerable spots? Yet I'm sprawled out in front of him now, nothing but a huge and pulsating open wound.

He seems to realize I need time to process. Time and space. Tilting his head toward the skinny tree, he says, "So, that one?"

"No," I say hoarsely. "Let's take the branch."

"Which branch?" This time, no skepticism or doubt. He looks ready to snap off any of the four branches on that sad little tree.

"Not those. The one in the road. I don't actually need a whole tree. I'm not putting any presents under it. I just like that pine smell."

"So you want to celebrate Christmas with the branch that almost killed me."

That dryly stated response *almost* makes me smile. "You'll get your revenge by dismembering it. And it's blocking part of the road, so it'll have to be cut down before we drive back through anyway."

"True." His dark eyes search my face. "What's the plan if the snow doesn't melt?"

"If I don't show up to work on the Monday after the new year, Harris sends a plow." That was just the plan for me, however. "Does anyone know where you are? Are you going to be listed as a missing person or return to attend your own funeral?"

"I sent Harris a text. I don't know if he replied. My phone's in there." He gestures to his pack. "He might have tried to tell me you were already here. Or…maybe he didn't."

"Because, in his opinion, it'd be hilarious if a blizzard

trapped us together?"

"Probably." He rubs his hand over his cold-reddened face, then gives me another of those warm looks. That caring look. "If it helps, it's not just your mom. My dad's a raging asshole, too."

"It does help." I don't know why, but it does. "What are you, Reed Knowles? Also a raging asshole?"

"Maybe." Then he shakes his head. "No, what I am is very lucky."

"True."

"No, I mean—I'm lucky I got whacked on the head. If I hadn't wrecked, I'd have stopped at the cabin, seen you were there, and left the same night. And I wouldn't have realized there's at least one Walker girl worth knowing. The Abbie girl."

"And I wouldn't have known my mother lied to me." Or that one Knowles man is maybe worth knowing, too.

This time when he offers his hand, I let him pull me to my feet. "What will you do now that you know?"

"I'm not sure yet." I swipe my gloves across my ass to brush off the snow. "Maybe there will be a Christmas miracle, and they'll have moved out before I get back."

"You think so?"

I sigh and shake my head. "I'm not the lucky one here."

"It's that bad?" he asks quietly.

"You really want to hear?"

"I'd like to know you better. Because if I'd bothered to know you before, maybe some of this shit would never have happened."

He's about to know me better than anyone else does, then. Because we're in a snowy wood with more than a mile to go, and I've never unloaded. I don't even realize how desperately I need to until I get started.

"Well, there's Lauryn, who's just...negative. Beyond, you know, normal bitching. It's as if nothing pleases her. If I take her out to dinner, the only comments she makes are about what's wrong—with the prices, with the food, with the service. But then she'll clean her plate. And I *know* her. When Lauryn doesn't like the way something tastes, she won't eat it. She'll ask me if I want it or leave it on her plate. So she enjoys it enough to finish, but what she enjoys is never mentioned. Only the negative stuff. Or if I say, 'Wow, this chocolate dessert is really good,' she'll comment that it looks like a piece of shit. *Every* time I mention something I like or enjoy, she'll find something wrong with it. I can barely stand to be around her anymore, because it's such a constant beatdown. And I keep my mouth shut about what I *do* enjoy now, so that she doesn't come swinging in with all her reasons why I *shouldn't* enjoy it. So I just feel...I don't know what."

"Silenced," Reed says, the sleeve of his coat brushing against mine as we walk, the sled sliding along behind.

"Yes? Not deliberately, because she hasn't *told* me to shut up. But I'm so tired of it. I don't want to deal with it anymore. There's this dread in my chest all the time when I'm with her, like I can't breathe. Nothing I do is good enough. Because she's also socially and environmentally conscious—which I get, and I'm on board for—"

"Me, too."

I don't know why I'm so glad to hear that, but I am. I pause, so distracted by his reply that I can't recall what I was explaining.

Reed saves me with a, "But she doesn't think your efforts are good enough?"

"Not even close. I *do* try to make responsible choices and to put my money where my mouth is. But I also accept that there are some things I just can't get around. So I choose what my priorities are, but there are areas where I have to make compromises. Mostly I just do my best as things come up."

"It's all anyone can do."

"Not if you're Lauryn. *Her* priorities are the right ones, *her* compromises are the acceptable ones. Everyone else gets judged for theirs. Oh! An example from just this past week: I've got a neighbor, Delia. She doesn't drive anymore—she's eighty, eighty-one?—and I check in on her when I can, and every once in a while she calls me if she needs help with something. So she asked me to pick up a few things from the grocery store—she gets them delivered, but sometimes the items she needs aren't in stock. So my sis is with me. And some of the things I get for Delia are these pre-sliced, pre-washed vegetables. Like diced onions. And Lauryn goes off on this, because of the wasteful packaging, how it's lazy because it doesn't take long to cut things up, and it's fresher if I get whole produce. So I have to tell her that Delia can't, because her arthritis is just bad enough that she can't grip her knife easily. So Lauryn says that I could cut them up for her—which I *have* done before—until I remind her that I'll be gone this week. But when I tell her that Delia wouldn't mind if my sister came over to do it, instead…yeah, nope."

Reed grunts and shakes his head, which I take as a complete lack of surprise at Lauryn's refusal to assist a neighbor.

"So anyway, Lauryn decided the packaged vegetables were okay—and I'm just, why does she feel like she gets to judge whether it's okay for Delia to use them? Why is it her place to judge? And why does Delia's personal business have to be laid out in the open, so that she can justify her choices to someone who shares no part of her life? But Lauryn does that all the time. She judges what people are doing—though, okay, we *all* judge other people. I'm judging Lauryn right now for all of her judgements! That's just human nature. But she judges, then doesn't ever ask herself why they might be doing it. She just decides they *must* be wrong—and then *says* they're wrong. Without making sure she's actually right. And without considering whether saying these things might give someone a bad name that's completely undeserved."

Reed clears his throat and bumps his arm lightly against mine. "I'm intimately familiar with the type of person who opens his mouth and says shit before he actually knows anything about the situation."

It's hard not to laugh. "At least you apologized."

"She doesn't?"

It's even harder not to laugh at that. "Somehow it was Delia's fault—or my fault—that Lauryn didn't know that Delia can't use a knife. Because Lauryn claims she wouldn't have said anything if she'd known. But why would I tell her? It wasn't any of her business. And it wasn't just that one time. She never apologizes for anything. Another example: when they moved in, while I was at work, Lauryn threw away half of what was in my fridge and pantry. Not even donated, but trashed it all—because she didn't like the brand, or she deemed it unacceptably sourced, or it had corn syrup in it, or GMOs—oh, she had reasons for it all. And when I yelled at her, she actually went on Reddit to ask if she was an asshole. And then she raged in the comments at all the people who said she was one, writing these long, long replies with the reasons *they* were wrong. Until finally a moderator came in and shut it down."

Reed's the one laughing now—his shoulders shaking and the deep sound of it rocketing through the trees.

"I *did* enjoy that," I have to admit. "I don't think she ever knew I saw the post and all the replies. And, god. I *wish* I could say her judging was always over important things, like the environmental stuff. Because at least there's something good at the core of it—wanting the world to be a better place. But it's the stupidest shit, too. Like you should have heard her a few months ago going off about pineapple on pizza. It's not my preference, but no one is forcing anyone else to eat it. Yet she talks about people who enjoy it as if it's a deep moral and ethical failing. And I'm not even joking when I say that if she had the power to forbid people from making it, she would. She'd do it for their own good, because they obviously don't know any better."

Reed grunts again. "Like washing legs."

"What?"

"It just reminds me of something I saw a while back online—about people who scrubbed their legs in the shower versus those who let the water run down and wash everything off. People were *invested* in this argument. A whole lot of them appalled and judging. But all I could think was, as long as no one's forcing anyone else to lick their legs, what the hell does it matter?"

"Right? Who's being hurt?"

"Sounds like you are," he says, looking over at me. "Not by pineapple or leg washing, but having to deal with similar shit all the time."

I sigh. Because that's the whole problem, isn't it?

"Is it just you or does Lauryn do the same thing at work? How does she get on with other people?"

"She doesn't work. My dad left her enough money that she can slide by as long as she lives with my mom—"

"Or you."

"Or me," I say unhappily. "I *have* pointed out that she can afford her own place if she gets a job—because she obviously isn't happy with the way I live—but there's always some excuse. Usually that most businesses are run by evil, greedy corporations. And I agree, some *are* evil. But not all of them. She could put in the effort to find like-minded people."

Reed frowns. "Wait. She'll toss *your* groceries because she doesn't like the brand or the ingredients—but does she use a smartphone? Or watch any streaming shows? Does she know those are all made by greedy corporations? And where does she keep her money? In a mattress? Because most banks are as greedy as they come."

"Right?! But like I said, *her* compromises are the acceptable ones. And it's not just corporations. Even a small business, there's always some problem that means she can't tolerate working there. She doesn't like where their product is sourced, or some policy they have, or there is an industry adjacent to the business that she can't approve of. Even a bookstore or library is out of the question."

Reed stops dead. "What?"

"Partially because they all carry books by people she doesn't think should have a platform. But also because the books use so much paper."

He looks like he's been whacked with another tree limb. "Okay, maybe the paper thing is true. But doesn't the good of a library outweigh the bad?"

"Nope. And there's always *some* issue, whatever it is. But when I say, 'If you work there you could find ways to change whatever you don't like or boost what you *do* like,' she always argues the business owners or the city or the current employees should have already done something—and if the policy is based on a law, they should already be fighting against the law. And I'm just…does she not know that people are *exhausted?* I see it every single day. People are just burned out and tired. And small businesses especially have no money to wage that kind of legal battle."

"You don't need to tell me," he says wryly.

"And it does no good to tell *her.* Any element of compassion or understanding seems to be chucked out the window, because she only cares about how things *should* be—but that's a level of idealism that's impossible to live up to if you participate in society at all. Yet for her, nothing else is acceptable. But what does she do to change anything or to help anyone? Nothing. All that energy she puts into criticizing everything around her could go into doing something at a ground level. But she doesn't. She doesn't even vote."

He grimaces. "If she truly cares about anything, that's the bare minimum." Then his brow furrows. "Why not work at a nonprofit like you do?"

"Oh, I suggested that, too. But we accept donations… from rich people and from corporations." It's hard not to smile when he laughs. "You should hear the snide shit she says about me working there."

Reed blinks at me in disbelief. Probably because he knows Harris's organization—which provides mental health and addiction services—was named one of the best nonprofits in the state to work for, several years running.

I shrug, because I don't understand either. "There's just nothing that she's satisfied with."

"And your mom's the same?"

"No." I sweep up another handful of snow, throw it at a tree trunk and watch powder explode everywhere. "To be fair, whatever else she is, my mom *does* put the work in. Maybe not for reasons that I can admire, but she does help people. But the problems between us mostly stem from her being so rooted in the past."

"The thing with your dad and my mom?"

"Well, also that. But mostly *my* past." I steal a glance up at him. He's still walking close, our arms brushing now and then. His head is tilted down toward me as if not wanting to miss a word—and I've said more words today than…maybe ever. Yet his attention hasn't strayed. "I don't remember this, but I was apparently a smart little kid. I was already reading and learning multiplication by the time I got to preschool. So she had plans for me, because she'd given up *her* dream to go to med school when she married my dad. And she made sure I was in the gifted programs, did the science camps, everything. But although I liked all those things, always got good grades, I was obsessed with drawing. Then painting. So when I started to push for more art classes and camps… well, you can imagine how that went. She belittled it. She would defend herself by saying that she wasn't belittling *me*, though that's how it felt. But she belittled art as a course of study—telling me that it wasn't even worth having as a hobby because I wasn't exactly a Picasso by middle school. So I would never stand out, which would be a sad, sad fate for someone with my potential—and she was just trying to guide me so I could be successful and never have to struggle or regret, like she did."

"Fuck her," Reed says harshly, then meets my eyes. "I know that pressure you're talking about. My dad did it differently, but he always wanted me to follow in his footsteps. And I like engineering, so I went along with his plans for a while. What I *don't* like is what he does. I don't want to spend my life building McMansions, even if there's money in it. That's his idea of a good life, not mine. But all it took was one shouting match and it was done with."

"Lucky you."

He smiles slightly. "Lucky me. He still suggests me joining him now and then, but he doesn't really care if I do. As long as he's got his. But your mom still brings it up—even now?"

"*All* the time. Or she'll randomly text pictures of me at science fairs as a kid. She'll say, 'Look at when you were so happy.' And the thing is…I wasn't. I liked learning everything but she was always more invested in it than I was. What *I* remember is trying so hard to make her happy and proud and never quite feeling like I did. And she has zero interest in who I am now. The only version of me she ever cared about was the one who represented all of her own hopes coming true. Or when I was the kid she could point to and say, 'Look how smart my daughter is'—because it reflected on *her* so well. Her texts should really say those pictures are from when *she* was so happy."

"Was this happy time before your dad died?"

"After. I was only seven when he was killed. Though when I was thinking about it a few years ago, I wondered if she'd thrown herself into securing my future as a reaction to his sudden death. I mean, I could understand that—even feel some sympathy for her. But…she's *still* doing it? Still trying to relive those happy years—and rewrite history so those were *my* happy years, too? She still does it, even though I'm secure and have a good job? But it's not a job that shines brightly enough, I guess. And she always suggests that Harris is doing me dirty, that he doesn't appreciate me enough and isn't paying me enough, but I'm doing *exactly* what I want to do and I'm happy with where I am. When I tell her that, though, or tell her to stop, she insists she's just trying to support me and make sure I get what I deserve. But really, she's just shitting on what I do and what I earn and all my friends." I let my head fall back and stare up at the clear blue sky. "Sometimes I wonder if she's punishing me. Maybe not even consciously, but punishing me for not becoming what she wanted me to be."

This time Reed's grunt has a rough edge. More like a growl. "Does she do the same to your sister?"

"Not really. If she sends Lauryn pictures, they're more likely to be pictures of my dad. He always did more stuff with Lauryn than with me—and she's older, so there are more photos of them together. But my mom and Lauryn, they kind of…circle around each other. They don't talk to each other much because they end up arguing, unless they're reminiscing about my dad. And when my mom *does* talk to her about other things, she's usually trying to push Lauryn into volunteering at MCS. Which, of course, is somewhere Lauryn would *never* go."

"MCS," Reed echoes, as if trying to place it. "That church school off Alder Road?"

"Yeah. Technically, a non-denominational Christian school. My mom began working there as one of the admin shortly after my dad was killed."

"Your sister didn't want to go to school there?"

"She was never given the option. Lauryn was already in the public school, and my mom decided it would be too upsetting for her to change. Now, of course—absolutely not. Lauryn won't touch anything so closely related to any church. But I didn't go there, either. I was only in second grade, so it wouldn't have really mattered if I'd changed schools… but my mom didn't think MCS offered the programs or facilities that I would need to reach my full potential. Not that she said so to anyone at the school who asked why we didn't enroll. I think she told them something about making a promise to my dad that we'd attend schools in our own neighborhoods. She always did stuff like that—use my dad as the reason behind whatever decision she made, because it's not as if anyone could verify the truth with him. As for the church part of it, my family didn't go before my dad died, and Lauryn and I didn't after."

"Your mom got religious after he died?"

"Yes? No?" I shrug. "That's the thing. If you ask anyone at that school, *anyone*—they will say she's the perfect model of charity and faith. She's nice to everyone, helps everyone. She gives so much of her time. And she does. She *does*. So it's hard, it's almost impossible to explain…it's all fake."

He makes a short, scoffing sound. As if once again, that's the least surprising thing he's heard. "It's organized religion. In my experience, what they preach and what they do are two very different things."

My experience is a little different. "I don't have much use for it, myself. But I know of some people who are genuine—we get a lot of overlap between the local churches and Harris's organization, and some of the people I meet truly, truly care. And MCS is on the more open-minded, welcoming end. No fire and brimstone and bigotry and misogyny. If there was, I honestly don't think I could have put up with my mom at all. So it's not like she wears a righteous face in public and spouts racism at home or something. She's not fake in the sense that she only pretends to help the people in that community. It's more like…the help she does is all for show. And I know that no one can really ever know what's inside someone—"

"But you see something different than what other people do."

I nod, my gaze on the road ahead. We've almost reached the hanging tree limb that hit him. "She volunteers for the school and puts on a smile…but at home, she complains about how much time she has to spend volunteering."

"Because nobody else will?"

"Because nobody else can do it *so well*. So she feels

obligated to do it. Otherwise it won't be done right."

Dryly Reed says, "And no one knows how she suffers."

"Oh, Lauryn and I know. My mom repeats every compliment she gets, and will tell us every time she's lauded—but more often, she's upset because she hasn't been complimented *enough*. They do thank her, she's frequently celebrated within the community—but not as much as she feels is deserved. What more she wants, I'm not sure. But she thinks she deserves more. That's what I mean when I say she's fake. She doesn't help people because it's good to help, but because it makes people say good things about her. And I suspect the *appearance* of being good is far more important to her than the actual good being done. Because she sure as hell never put in any similar effort at home."

"What do you mean by— No. Hold that thought. Let me get the saw."

Because we've reached the branch. The broken part of the bough hangs almost vertically toward the road, like giant, bushy tail. Above our heads, the limb has split horizontally, and the broken end is still attached with a strip of what resembles a three-inch-thick tendon of fir.

That tendon will be the best place to cut, but it's out of his reach, even with the additional eighteen inches offered by the hacksaw blade.

"This must be one of the first times in your life you're not tall enough to do something." I pat his shoulder. "But I believe in you. You're a structural engineer. Surely you'll build a ladder out of twigs."

He casts me a look that says my innocent tone hasn't fooled him. "Yeah, and what my fancy degree tells me is that the wood is too green to snap, and I'm also not strong or heavy enough to rip it free." Reed eyes the limb again, then nods. "All right. I can't get up there. We'll bring it down here. Hold this saw and step back for a few minutes."

I do, watching as he plants his boot on the end of the dangling bough, pushing it down toward the snow. Then stepping again, a little higher along the branch, forcing that section down into the snow. It almost looks like he's trying to climb the bough like a ladder...but his weight is bringing it down, instead. The limb creaks overhead—then screeches, as the split deepens.

"You *are* ripping it free," I tell him.

He shakes his head. "It's only ripping along the grain. It'll stop where that limb gets thicker. But then the whole thing should start bending."

I look at it again, realize what he means. "And then we'll have a catapult. Too bad there's no nearby castle to breach."

He huffs out one of his dry laughs, stepping higher up the bough—and the bough comes down farther. "You do realize it would be catapulting me?"

"That would be the whole point," I say, though I hadn't realized. "You breach the castle and fight everyone with your bare hands. Will my weight help keep it down?"

"It's not a worry. This thing isn't throwing me anywhere. And when it gets low enough, I'll have you saw—because the more tension in that limb up there, the more unsteady this end of the branch will be. Since I'm standing on it, it'd be a bad idea to start sawing it myself."

"All right. Anything I can do now?"

"Yeah. Tell me what you meant by your mom not making the effort. You're talking about when you were kids?"

"Mostly." I'm a little distracted watching the limb overhead begin to bend. "Because that's when it matters most, right?"

"Probably. Was this after you started pursuing art? Because it sounds like before that she was pretty damn involved, pushing you where she wanted you to be."

"She did both, weirdly. Pushed me and also didn't make the effort. Looking back, it makes more sense to me now. Pushing me was really for *her*. So she put in effort. But anything else that was just for Lauryn and me, like showing up for volleyball games or our track meets, or school plays, or birthdays—or Christmas. It was just, nope. She was busy—not at her job, really, but with all the related volunteering."

He pauses and spears me with an intense look. "She didn't do Christmas?"

"Not after Dad died. But again, I thought it was the grief. At first."

"Ours was different after my mom, too. We had all the stuff—the tree, the nice dinner, and my dad would spend a shitload on my presents—but I can't say there was any joy in it anymore."

An unexpected pang strikes my heart as I imagine a younger Reed surrounded by gifts but lacking the sweetest part of Christmas. And *knowing* he was lacking it. "The first few years, my grandparents showed up for a little while on Christmas Eve and brought stuff—my dad's parents. Then my mom had a falling out with that side of the family. I don't know why. But I haven't seen them in a long time. My grandpa on her side, I never met. And her mom, my grandma…I get the feeling she's a lot like my mom is. Not putting in effort unless it benefits her personally or makes her look good. She remarried and has another set of grandkids anyway."

"Did she ever explain why it changed? Christmas, I mean."

"She *said* it was because the holidays had all become too fake and commercialized—and that the true meaning of Christmas got buried under all the tinsel and wrapping paper. Which is true, but a lot of people don't celebrate it for the religious aspect anyway. Instead they get together for…I don't know, togetherness. That's how we celebrated when my dad was alive. But after, even togetherness wasn't reason enough. And not just for the holidays. Any day. If we needed her to attend something, Mom always had something else to do, something more important. She was always busy. Because she never said no to the school and always said no to us. But even when she didn't have an event scheduled, she'd say that she was too tired after being so busy. Which might have been true, but we learned really quickly we weren't worth her time—or any money. So it was like she used the school as justification for being as uncaring and uncharitable as possible toward her own family."

"I suspect Baby Jesus would not approve."

Oh shit. He almost got me there. I have to bite my lips to stop my laugh.

He narrows his eyes, watching me. Then he shakes his head and continues forcing down the limb.

"Maybe the money issue was real, though," I continue, turning all the new information over in my head. "After all, she wasn't paying the taxes. And she had money from Dad, too, but I know at least some of it went to pay off the mortgage. Maybe the mortgage took more than I realized."

Reed mutters something that I don't quite catch.

"What?"

He pauses again, and the look in his eyes is a lot like when he told me about the fifteen years of unpaid taxes. "I said she probably spent it on lawyers."

"What do you mean?"

"She sued my mom for malpractice."

"How?" The money I'm talking about was spent *after* my dad died—and so after his mom died, too. "How did she sue your mom after she was dead?"

"She went after the value of her practice. Since my mom was your dad's psychiatrist."

I gape at him. "She did what? I can hardly...yet it makes so much sense! I've heard all my life how unethical your mom was"—a flash of pain in his expression stops me cold—"I'm sorry, I didn't mean to—"

"No," he says firmly. "It *was* unethical to hook up with her patient." A smile quirks the side of his mouth. "Do you know how often I heard my father call your dad a slippery two-faced hypocrite?"

"Oh, I know that one." It's not anything that I haven't silently acknowledged myself. "He was a good man, one of the few honest lawyers and politicians left, an upright pillar for justice. My mom can go on forever talking about what a paragon he was. Obviously only an unethical Jezebel could have made him stray—and so it was all your mom's fault, not his. He was emotionally manipulated by an expert into abandoning his children and family, because he would *never* have broken his vows otherwise."

Reed gives me another wry look. "Neither one was an angel, were they?"

I shake my head.

"All right." With an upward jerk of his chin, he says, "Try sawing it now. But stand off to the side as much as you can, because that limb will snap upward but this branch is going down hard."

Nodding, I lift the blade and just manage to reach the tendon. I begin sawing—and the back and forth, back and forth reminds me far too much of *rubbing*. And of the last time I rubbed something. Oh god. I nearly burst into hysterical giggles but somehow stop myself.

And my mother is always a topic that can sober me up. "Do you think one lawsuit would be that expensive?" I'm already panting and my arms are aching from having to saw overhead like this. "If that's where all her money went?"

"Not one lawsuit. She went after my mom for years.

Filed multiple lawsuits."

I shoot him a horrified glance. "Multiple?"

"Her lawyer came at it from about every conceivable angle until the courts said he'd be sanctioned if they filed another suit. I remember my dad crowing about that, too. You all right? Want to take a rest?"

"No," I gasp, though my shoulders are on fire. I'm afraid if I stop now, I won't be able to lift the saw high enough again. "So she went…after the money. Though she always said…*you* were the immoral…cheats. All the while…it was the money."

"While my dad always said you were all goody-goody hypocrites who never did an actual good thing, you just threw shit to stain other people's names. Not that my dad did any good. Unless it was tax deductible. But he never *claimed* to be good, so I guess— *Get back!*"

I stumble backward and take another tumble onto my ass. The limb whips upward. Reed slams full-length to the ground, carried down by the freed end of the bough. A cloud of icy powder bursts into my face from the impact. I brush it away with gloves that are just as covered in snow, spitting and shaking my head.

Reed groans. He's still face down, spreadeagled across a bed of green needles.

"Did the mean branch hurt you again?" I ask him. "Are you dying inside?"

"No, I'm doing great." With another groan, he rolls onto his side. "Just going to stay here for a second, though."

I crawl over and lie on my side facing him. He hasn't opened his eyes yet, but a quick scan of his body doesn't reveal anything that looks worse than it did before. "If you're broken, I'll pull you back on the sled. It's the least I can do after you bravely captured your attempted murderer while in hot pursuit of a Christmas tree."

His slow smile reminds me of the one he wore in his delirium. "I'm not broken."

"I'm glad, because I bet you're heavy. Do you know what I was thinking, just before the branch snapped? It might be terrible to say."

He opens his eyes, his gaze sharp. Focused. So no new head injury. No delirium. "Tell me anyway."

"I was thinking that it was no surprise that my dad left my mother. I can't agree with the way he did it, abandoning me and my sister. And there's no excuse for cheating. But escaping my mom? I get it."

"Heh. I've never blamed my mom for leaving my dad, either. I sure as fuck couldn't live with him." His expression softens. "This time, *you* had to escape."

"It's not the first time I did—though things weren't *as* bad before. But I was out of there after high school. Started doing things I wanted to do. Including Christmas, though that was just one thing of many. Escaping here…it's not really about Christmas at all."

"No?"

"No. I *could* have stayed and did all kinds of Christmassy stuff. After I started working for Harris, I've mostly spent the holidays backing him up at work events and charity fundraisers, though I also did the tree and lights and all that at my house. And I *like* the season, don't get me wrong, but celebrating at home wasn't super important. Last year, though…it was all the shit from when I was a kid all over again. But worse, because I knew what freedom was like. And this year…I just couldn't bear the thought of being there. Every night after work, the last year and a half, I'd come home to them, and it seemed like everything good and happy inside me was being sucked away. I just didn't have enough left for anyone else. Even the usual stuff with Harris was sucking everything away, too. But it could have been *any* time of year. I just…hit my limit. So I decided to do this for myself. Just for myself. Does that sound selfish?"

"No. Selfish is when it deliberately hurts someone who doesn't deserve to be hurt. You're not hurting anyone." His warm gaze searches my face. "You say you're usually with Harris over the holidays, but that's work. What about other friends?"

"They're mostly all from work, too. But even them… there's no one I'm *that* close to. It's difficult being so open with someone." Yet, here I am. Lying on a branch in the snow, spilling my guts to Reed Knowles.

His brow arches as if he had a similar thought. *Yet, here she is.* "Then I'll be your friend."

I'm always blindsided with him. "You can't. We're already sworn enemies."

"A sworn enemy here to ruin your Christmas," he says

with a little grin. "Now tell me what your perfect Christmas looks like so I know what to ruin."

Warmth spills through me. I know he's not asking to ruin it. He wants to know so that he can help me have it. "Honestly, there's nothing in particular. I got all of the dinner trappings, but mostly because I could and I wanted to cook." I finger the fir needles flattened in front of me. "I don't care about the tree specifically, but I do love the smell and how the greenery looks. Mostly I just wanted to enjoy something without being made to feel like shit for enjoying it."

"And you thought, with someone named Knowles around, I'd be one more person tearing you down."

My throat thick, I whisper, "Yes."

"I'll promise you this, Abbie." He traces my cheek with a gloved finger while his gaze holds mine. "Nothing I ever say will be *meant* to hurt you. If you aren't sure how to take something, ask me. Yeah? And I'll make sure you get the Christmas you need."

My eyes blur and I nod. But I refuse to cry again. I blink away the welling tears and find his gaze on my mouth. My stomach tightens. Is he thinking of kissing me?

Do I *want* him to kiss me? Just because he's been so unexpectedly nice?

It would be *more* nice of him to kiss me. Though maybe a little rough, with all that stubble shadowing his jaw. It's almost heavy enough now to be called a beard, framing his mouth and emphasizing the firm shape of his lips.

"Abbie?"

"Hmm?" I say, a little distracted because his stubble is good hairy. And I don't mind rough. Rough can be very, *very* nice.

"I'm going to kiss you tomorrow."

My heart gives a wild thump. Then— "Tomorrow?"

"Yes." He's wearing that little smile again.

"What's wrong with now?"

"I want you to think about it for a while first."

"As some kind of torture?" I narrow my eyes. "This is why we'll remain enemies."

His grin widens. "You *want* me to kiss you now?"

"Hardly." With a dramatic sigh, I flop onto my back. "But if you do it tomorrow, I'm sure to be disappointed after so much buildup. How can reality live up to the anticipation?"

"But you *are* anticipating it." His smug tone is absolutely infuriating.

"Not anymore. I just said it's destined to disappoint. Why would I anticipate a disappointing kiss?"

"You realize now I *have* to wait until tomorrow. To prove you wrong."

"If proving me wrong is more important than kissing, you're definitely staying an enemy."

"You are the most—"

Whatever I'm the most of, Reed doesn't say. Instead he breaks off with a frustrated growl low in his throat—sounding a little werewolf-y, which is also good hairy. Then suddenly he's over me, forearms braced alongside my shoulders and his hips wedged between my thighs. The feel of his stiffened length through the bulk of his snow suit steals my breath, though he's not moving, not rubbing, not kissing me. His head lowers, but not mouth to mouth. Instead he rests his forehead against mine…or more accurately, since we're bundled up, his knit cap against mine.

"It's my turn to take care of you, Abbie," he says, his voice roughened by the intensity of that declaration, his breath warming my lips. "And you told me that you're never usually open. But you were ripped wide open today—and I won't take advantage of you being vulnerable. I'd fucking hate myself if I did. If we kiss now and you regretted it tomorrow, we'll be stuck in that cabin together, both of us feeling like shit for doing something we wish we could undo. So *that's* what I want you to think about. Not the kiss, but whether you're sure. You say no, that's fine. I'll understand. But if you're sure tomorrow, I'll kiss you. All right?"

I nod, my knit cap rubbing against his, my throat aching with emotion. Because here's what I just learned about Reed Knowles: he's not nice. He's *kind.* Which is a million times better.

"All right," I tell him. And for the first time in a long time, it actually feels as if everything *will* be all right. Maybe not this minute. But somehow, someday.

Maybe even soon.

Abbie

AFTER ALL THAT, BARELY ANOTHER WORD PASSES BETWEEN us on the way back. Me, because I'm utterly wiped out—emotionally, physically. Reed, because his leg is hurting him. Not that he says so. But his limp is worse and he seems completely focused on reaching the cabin.

I'm not so focused. I'm drained, but my thoughts are all over the place. I'm also…lighter. Not like I was before, when I first stepped outside and it felt as if that heavy weight retreated for a while. This time, it feels as if I've left that weight behind. Maybe because I unloaded on Reed. But considering everything I discovered, shouldn't I be sad and grieving? Or angry? My own mother lied to me, betrayed my trust, and used me. But beyond the initial shock and hurt, mostly I feel *relief*.

I don't know how or why. But maybe I'll eventually talk to Reed about it.

Talk to Reed Knowles.

Who even *am* I now? I can hardly comprehend the one-eighty that I've gone through with him. Am I really such a sucker for a bit of kindness? I don't *think* I am.

Regardless, I can't regret anything I said to him.

I probably should have talked to someone about all of this before, because putting my experiences into words ordered so many of my thoughts and helped clarify so many of my emotions. The irony is, at work I see the benefits of counseling all the time. Yet I never considered it for my own situation. Whenever I articulated my complaints to myself, the issues always sounded so petty and ridiculous—and I feared being told that I was too sensitive or thin-skinned, especially when so many people have actual, serious problems. Because what would I say? I've got an older sister who picks on me. I've got a mother who volunteers too much. It seemed too embarrassing to describe to anyone how much they've hurt me. Just like it was too embarrassing to ever tell anyone how much I hate going home. So I never mentioned any of it to anyone else.

Yet I wasn't embarrassed while telling Reed. And with my memories laid out for me to examine all together, the hurt doesn't seem so petty or ridiculous after all.

It also made me realize how much more hurt I am by Lauryn than my mom. Perhaps because I simply don't have as many positive memories of my mother. But my sister and I used to be closer. Lauryn wasn't always so negative. Not when we were kids or teenagers. Then there was a period of about seven years—which included graduations and college, and me moving out of my mom's house—when we didn't see each other very often. Either Lauryn wasn't as bad during those seven years or I didn't notice how judgy she'd become because our meetings were so infrequent. It wasn't until after she moved in that the endless negativity and criticism began wearing me down.

And the thing is, I understand a lot of it. The world is shitty in so many ways. I understand the anger, the discontent.

But there are also so many people who can't push back against the shit. Because they don't have time or money; or they don't have the spoons, emotionally and mentally and physically. So they can't devote themselves toward changing things. But Lauryn could.

She just doesn't. And I've judged her for it...but I've never asked myself *why* she doesn't. Not to excuse her, but to at least understand.

Until today, I'd forgotten how she'd been considered my dad's kid, while I was my mom's. And although I've always thought of us both as having been abandoned—by my dad leaving and my mom not making the effort—in a way, Lauryn was *more* abandoned than I was. My mom had her plans for me, and from Lauryn's perspective, that must have seemed like positive attention. Perhaps it's no wonder that Lauryn tries so hard to do what's right and good. She might have been trying to gain a little bit of the attention my mom spent on me.

I don't think she's trying to get my mom's attention now.

That ship has sailed. But that doesn't mean she didn't learn some things from our mother—including the negativity and nitpicking. My mom is just more subtle about it.

But my mom also projects this image of (goody goody) perfection. She does everything for the right reasons. She tries to do what's best for everyone else. She always sacrifices her own time and interests on behalf of a greater cause. And I can see Lauryn trying to do what's right and to be perfect in her own way.

Doing right is one thing, however. Trying to be perfect is another. One of the first things I learned from my art instructors was that perfection is the enemy of progress. No piece would ever be finished if it had to be absolutely perfect. It would be an endless toil of trying and trying and trying, yet never reaching the goal.

Maybe that's what happened to Lauryn. Maybe she's paralyzed by the impossibility of being perfect. Maybe the pressure to do everything right means never taking a step for fear it might be the wrong one—as if there's a pitfall waiting behind every shining door. And I suppose there is. Because nothing is ever completely, perfectly right.

Maybe she's so worried about stepping wrong in her quest to do right, she's lost sight of what truly matters—which is the people around her.

Then again, maybe that's only what matters to *me*, not to Lauryn. I hope that's not true. Because it's what frustrates me most about her—feeling as if she completely forgets about people. Both the people who need help and the people who are helping. She's so focused on pointing at all the wrong things in the world, it's like she's blind to the efforts people are making to right those wrongs. And when she's not blind to the effort, she criticizes the effort because the results aren't perfect. Maybe that's what makes me so angry with Lauryn now. To see so many people working, and trying, and doing their best, and to have her dismiss those effort as shit. As never good enough.

Because I'm also doing my best. Yet I'm never good enough for her. For my own sister. Who's been where I've been, who has lived through much of the same shit as I have, the same grief and loss, who grew up with the same mom. Everything I do isn't enough for the one person in the world who *should* understand me.

It's also bewildering to realize…that one person in the world might actually be Reed Knowles.

Who will kiss me tomorrow. If I want him to.

But not *just* a kiss. I know that. Reed must, too. It wouldn't ever stop at a kiss. Not with the two of us stuck in the cabin together. Not when there's only one bed. Not when I keep thinking about his dick. *Just* kisses might last…a day? An hour?

Five fucking minutes?

It's almost unfathomable that kissing him is even a question. A day ago—hell, only this morning—I wouldn't have considered it. Not for a second.

Yet I see him so differently now. Even the worst thing I thought about him—the bulldozing of my mother's house—seems a little more understandable after hearing that my mom spent years suing his dead mother. Honestly, I'm not sure there's much difference between how awful our surviving parents are. They each wanted to destroy everything the other one had. Reed's father just happened to be more successful. Though my mom didn't make out too badly, either (except I'd bet anything that four hundred thousand isn't as much as my mother thought she deserved, so she probably *does* feel that Knowles cheated her).

Pushing all that old family feud crap aside, however, the only reason I disliked Reed Knowles was because of the shit he said to Harris. There was no excuse for that. But I am impressed with how he'd owned it and apologized.

Am I too easily impressed? Are my standards too low? I don't think so. If he'd really been as terrible as I believed he was, then yes—my forgiveness came too easily. But on top of everything I discovered today is the undebatable fact that *I did not know him.* I essentially met Reed Knowles the night he stumbled into the cabin. What I've learned of him since...I like. A lot.

I also like his declaration that he'd never intentionally hurt me.

But should I trust it?

I think I might. Because I don't know Reed well, but I do know my boss. Harris O'Neil doesn't keep friends unless he respects them—and Reed is his closest friend. I've known *that* for a long time...yet I dismissed how their friendship suggested that Reed wasn't as bad as I'd believed him to be, because it didn't fit the narrative I *knew* was true.

But slap my ass and call me Jon Snow, because it turns out I knew nothing at all.

BY THE TIME WE REACH the cabin, only one thought remains in my head. Not Lauryn, not my mother's lies, not Reed and whether to (not *just*) kiss him. No, that one thought is: *food.*

Thanks to my multiple tumbles into the snow, my fleece-lined leggings are wet up the ass. I strip naked in the bathroom, hang my underwear and leggings to dry, and change into my coziest sweats. Reed must have also done a quick-change. When I come out, his pack is open and he's wearing faded jeans with a blue fisherman sweater. The sweater's sleeves are pushed halfway up his forearms, which is utterly freaking ridiculous. How dare he? All he needs is a pocketknife and an apple and I'd be in a drooling puddle at his feet. Luckily for me, he's got a bow saw and a tree bough instead, and I'm so hungry that it doesn't matter how mouthwatering his hands and forearms are. My belly needs fed.

The charcuterie board takes a little longer than usual to assemble, probably because I'm cramming half of everything into my mouth before it reaches the platter. By the time I set it on the table, my belly beast has been tamed, and Reed has dismembered half the limb.

Overall the broken section of the bough is the length of a tall Christmas tree, but the secondary branches extend out flat on two sides instead of all around. Only those smaller branches are bushy with needles, so Reed saws his way down the broken bough like he's removing ribs from a spine. When done, he drags the denuded limb outside, and if my mouth wasn't full of cheese, I'd have joked that he managed to whittle a bear-hunting spear after all.

He returns just as I'm pulling the mini sausage rolls from the oven. Like a dumbass, he snatches one up, then hisses and tosses the hot weenie from hand to hand waiting for it to cool.

So stupid. But his forearms are still exposed by his pushed-up sleeves, and his hands are so big—and the flex of tendon and muscle so mesmerizing—I can almost forgive the dumbassery.

Finally he pops the sausage roll into his mouth, then gestures to the pile of greenery. "Do you want help decorating?"

"I don't *need* help," I say, hoping he doesn't have his own festive vision of how the cabin will look. "But do you *want* to help? If so, you can."

"I won't pretend it's a favorite pastime, but I *will* help you. Happily."

That response allows me to fully forgive the dumbassery. "Then no, I'd rather do it myself."

"All right. But if you need me to hold something in place, I'm your man." Reed's a quick learner, apparently, because he goes for the not-piping-hot charcuterie board next. "Do you mind if I write while you decorate?"

"Not at all." Those sleeves are still up, so watching him type while I labor away will be an extra Christmas Eve treat.

He heads for his pack. From it he pulls a pair of over-the-ear headphones, then casts an apologetic glance my direction. "White noise helps me focus."

Ah. So he's letting me know that his intention isn't to be a rude asshole like I was yesterday with my earbuds. "All right." A thought strikes me. "Are they noise cancelling? Do you care if I play Christmas music?"

"Go to. If you need anything, just wave in my face."

I practically skip over to grab my Bluetooth speaker and phone. By the time I've got it set up, Reed has loaded a plate and is settled down at the table in front of…something that's not a laptop. Not a typewriter, either. I don't know what it is. It almost looks like a giant, extra-wide calculator—but instead of a number pad, it's got a full-sized keyboard.

I wave my hand in front of his face. Eyebrows raised, he pulls the headphones down.

I point. "What in the holy name of Radio Shack *is* that?"

Reed grins. "This is my baby," he says, and actually caresses the dark green casing. "It's an AlphaSmart Neo."

"It looks as old as I am."

"Not quite. Though maybe close. They stopped making them more than a decade ago. I bought this one online the first time I came out here to the cabin, and I've picked up a few more since then, in case it dies. This one has lasted me about eight years so far, though."

"But…why not a laptop? Or a tablet?"

"Because this gets seven hundred hours of run time on three AA batteries."

"Hours? Seven *hundred* hours?"

He nods. "And it'll hold about two hundred pages—around half of one of my books."

Oh. "So out here in the middle of nowhere and with no electricity…"

"I can spend a few weeks. I *do* have a laptop with me so I can clear out the Neo's memory and back up my work, but I save that battery just for the transfer."

I shake my head, cringing inside at the thought of trusting some ancient machine that was discontinued years ago not to erase half a book. But it's apparently worked for him this long. Although… "Is your head healed enough now to read on that tiny display?"

"I only had to change the settings a bit." Turning the device toward me, he shows me the little LCD screen… and the *enormous* font.

Oh shit.

Suddenly he looks entirely too pleased with himself. "You almost laughed."

"But I didn't." I snag a jalapeño popper so that I'll have something in my mouth to stifle my giggles if I think about that font size again. Breezily I add, "You may carry on now. Thank you for indulging my curiosity."

"My pleasure," Reed says, smiling as he puts his headphones on again.

I get started on the decorations, humming along with the carols—sometimes singing quietly since he can't hear me—and nearly high on the fresh scent of pine. Most of the branches end up on the fireplace mantel, but I hang others above the shutters and door—then save one for the bathroom, because Hot Biscuit Slim seems to be over his digestion issues, but that little space can use the extra pine odor protection.

All of the greenery gets draped in cranberry and popcorn garlands. By the end, the cabin is ridiculously festive and cheery, and I absolutely love it. I settle into my armchair to bask.

Then I remember Reed's forearms.

He's very, very focused on that little screen. Now and again he'll grab a bite from his plate without looking away, rub his fingers on a napkin, and get back to typing. I don't know what he's working on, exactly, but his expression makes fascinating changes as he goes—as if he's subconsciously mirroring whatever his characters are thinking or feeling as he writes them down. And his posture isn't *tense*, yet he sits forward in the chair, and instead of letting his feet rest flat on the floor, his lower legs are balanced on the balls of his feet, as if he's on the verge of standing. Overall there's just an intensity to Reed's whole being as he works that I find incredibly appealing. Before too long, my fingers itch to dig out my sketchpad and capture him in long, strong strokes.

Or...I can paint. He promised not to say anything to hurt me. I either trust that or I don't.

I do. Mostly.

I set up my easel behind the armchairs—which is also the small open space at the end of the bed—where he'd have to deliberately come looking to see what I'm working on. No accidental peeks from this angle. Not that he's noticed what I'm doing. The man truly does focus. But when I haul a canvas out of my large tote, *that* gets his attention.

His headphones come down around his neck. I say nothing.

Reed watches me lay out my brushes on top of the dresser—which turns out to be a very convenient workspace—and as I squirt paint onto my palette. Finally he says, "You know I want to look. But I'll wait for an invitation."

That was the kindest, sweetest thing he could have said. But I only reply, "You'll be waiting a while."

He grins. And doesn't return to his work. He just stares at me.

"What?" I ask warily.

"You smiled."

"No, I didn't." Oh god, maybe I did. His reply truly made me happy. "Did I?'

"You did."

Shit. But I shrug. "It's another Christmas miracle, I guess." And at least I didn't laugh.

"Another?"

Reed saying 'thank you' and complimenting my soup were the other miracles. Those seem too petty to tell him now. "You making it here alive seems like one."

His grin widens. "You wouldn't have called that a miracle a few days ago. More like a curse."

"I'm *trying* to be nice. Since it's Christmas Eve. Now

hush your mouth and let me paint."

"Yes, ma'am." Up go his headphones, but he's still grinning and casting glances my way.

I try to ignore him. But oh, it's hard. Because he's big and intense and smells like pine—and he's kind. So who wants to climb him like he's a giant Christmas tree?

Surprise, surprise. It's me.

THE END OF THE DAY comes early and hits me hard. By the time I'm out of the shower and braid my hair, my entire body is dragging. Reed's taking his own shower when I finally crawl under the covers…where I lie awake, shivering and utterly exhausted, but with my brain in the grip of nervous anticipation. Because although there won't be any kissing until tomorrow, the blood rushing through my veins can't tell time. Add in the knowledge that he'll soon be in bed with me, there's no hope yet of sleeping.

Then he comes out of the bathroom, and the blood in my veins says the time should be now. Right now.

Because he shaved. *Shaved.* I'd bet five bucks that he usually lets his beard grow wild when he's at the cabin. But instead he shaved his jaw smooth. As if he's planning to do something with his face soon and doesn't want his stubble tearing up delicate skin while doing it.

I'm not sleepy anymore. I might never sleep again. I know Reed won't go back on his timeline. Not when he's worried about taking advantage of me. Nothing will happen until tomorrow.

But he's *preparing* for something to happen. And I can't tell him that my body is already ready. I wouldn't mind torturing him, but I don't want to torture myself.

Watching him is torture enough. Wearing only pajama pants, he makes his way around the cabin—checking the stove, throwing more wood on the fire, flipping the deadbolt (as if another abominable snowman will find his way to the door.) The flickering firelight dances over his skin as he returns to the bed, illuminating his rough hairy body and his hard smooth jaw, turning every part of him into a delicious play of textures and angles, light and shadow.

Maybe he assumes I'm already sleeping, because he doesn't say anything before climbing in. I'm lying on my side facing the center of the bed, watching as he settles back against his pillow and closes his eyes. Not even a glance in my direction.

Well…fuck him.

I screw my eyes shut. Everything's quiet.

Then out of nowhere he says, "Next time, I'll make you laugh."

Which makes me laugh. I try to stop it, burying my face in my pillow. Too late.

"YES!" Reed crows, coming up onto his elbows. "I win our battle of skill and wits."

It takes me a second to remember what he's referring to. Of course I can't give an inch. "That's only in a fight with friends. Not enemies."

With a disgruntled "Dammit, Abbie," he flops back down

and turns onto his side, arm cocked and head propped on his hand, biceps flexed, eyes narrowed. "After everything you learned today, why do we still have to be enemies? None of your reasons had any solid factual basis."

"You *did* say that shit to Harris."

"You forgave me."

"Did I?" I'm trying *so* hard not to smile.

"Yeah, you did," he says confidently. "And not that it made any difference, since he knew I was being a dick and hired you anyway. What *do* you do for him?"

"I'm the Director of Community Engagement and Development." I say the job title like a grand pronouncement before adding, "Which just means I'm in charge of the organization's messaging and social media—and finding new avenues for donations. Though I don't have to do the face-to-face fundraising myself, thankfully, because I'm not that personable."

"Because you're too blunt? Or because you like making enemies out of perfectly harmless men who interrupt your solitary holidays?"

"Probably the first." And he's got me smiling again. "I do develop the talking points for the others to use while they're fundraising, though."

"So, marketing."

"That's what my degree is in."

His brows draw in, as if he's contemplating a puzzle. His eyes search my face through the flickering darkness. "And do you enjoy that? Marketing?"

"I do. I like figuring out what makes people interested or invested, and working out how I can convince others to care. But mostly because it involves so much graphic design—which was my other major."

"Ah," he says, as if something clicks into place. "And the painting—is that something you do professionally or just for fun?"

"I have a side gig. That's what I'm working on here. But it's not for the money, because there's not much money in it. I just enjoy it," I say, then sigh.

Reed's beginning to read me too easily, because he asks, "But not enjoying it lately?"

"Not at home, no. I'm told how pointless and silly it is—and that I'm not good enough to make a career of it, so why bother?"

A soft growl sounds in his throat. "Even if it's silly as fuck and never makes a cent, I have no patience for anyone who shits on what other people enjoy. Especially when those things aren't hurting anyone else."

"Oh, you need to talk to Lauryn. We *are* hurting people by selling our work. All art and intellectual property should be freely distributed to everyone, so even if I do create something pretty now and then, I shouldn't feel entitled to be paid for it."

He groans. "She's one of *those*?"

I have to laugh, because the pain is real. "You get them, too, with your books?"

"All the time."

"And told we'll be replaced by artificial intelligence?"

"Even worse." He reaches out, and my heart thunders as he brushes the side of his thumb down my cheek. "Are we truly still enemies?"

How can he keep blindsiding me like this? "We *should* be," I answer breathlessly. "Tradition, and all that. I can't befriend a Knowles man. After all these years, it's almost… blasphemy. And you know I'm too goody goody to sin."

His gaze slips down to my mouth. "Maybe we'll find out tomorrow how goody goody you—"

He jerks back, sucking air through his teeth in a curse as Hot Biscuit Slim claws his way onto the bed, not caring that Reed's bare skin is in his path.

Reed catches him. "Fucking Christ. I ought to throw you into a snowbank, you mangy rat!"

I'd take that a little more seriously if Reed wasn't already sitting up, cradling the cat against his broad chest and rubbing his ears. Hot Biscuit Slim, of course, is purring. Loudly.

The traitor.

"He actually likes you, you know." And it doesn't make me jealous *at all*. "He never curls up on my lap like he does yours."

"You can curl up on my lap anytime, too. Whether you like me or not."

Leaning forward, he sets Hot Biscuit Slim down near our feet, then stretches out on his side again, but closer— and at exactly the same time I'm stifling a yawn against the back of my hand.

His dark gaze sweeps my face. "Did you sleep last night?"

I shake my head, already yawning again.

"Me neither. I spent all night thinking that I should have apologized for what I said to Harris. I should've just talked to you."

"Not sure I would have answered you yesterday," I admit drowsily. "I hated you too much."

He huffs a short laugh.

I eye him. "What?"

"You always say what you mean. I like that about you. I like it a lot."

"Even when what I'm saying isn't so nice?"

"Maybe especially then. Because you've made me rethink some things, Abbie Walker."

"What things?" I ask and have to cover my mouth again.

"I'll tell you later, because that's the fourth time you've yawned in as many minutes."

"I *am* tired," I confess. "Someone crashed his snowmobile really far away from the cabin so I had to hike miles and miles through the snow."

"Uphill both ways?"

"Seemed like it." Without forethought, I turn around and snuggle back against his chest. "Is this okay? You're really warm and it feels nice."

"Yeah," he says quietly, his voice deeper than before. "Is *this* okay?"

His arm drapes over my side and he pulls me in tighter.

I sigh contentedly. "It is. Although if tonight is anything

like the other night, we'll both roll around. We might end up where we ought to be."

"Where should we be?"

"Apart. Like enemies."

"You don't believe in keeping enemies close?"

"No. Though I do believe in using my enemies to protect my tits from Hot Biscuit Slim."

A short laugh rumbles from him. Then he seems to slowly go still behind me. As if bracing himself. "Did you decide for tomorrow?"

"Yes."

"And?"

"Yes."

That stillness recedes. He drags me even closer, spooning his full length behind mine—and although I'm a teaspoon and he's a big serving spoon, somehow it works. "So there's no mistaking, I dying to get my mouth on you *now*. Not tomorrow. But I won't take advantage when you're exhausted, either. Not the first time."

His words shiver over my skin...but I have to admit to some disappointment. Because I can feel him behind me, the bulge of his cock—but he's not erect. Semi-hard, at best.

I wiggle my ass against him. "Honestly, I'm not getting interest from you. Certainly no dying."

Wryly he replies, "Probably because I jerked off in the shower."

Oh. Well, okay. That's much better. "Did you?"

"Twice."

"Twice?" Impressive. His shower lasted maybe fifteen minutes. "So you have decent recovery time."

"Only because I have a very strong imagination, and I can't stop thinking about getting inside you."

My inner muscles clench. "I see. Is now a good time to confess that I masturbated while you were sleeping beside me the other night?"

"It's always a good time to confess something like that." He exhales a long breath, then seems to hold the next. "Were you thinking of me?"

"You might have been pounding me into the mattress at one point, with my ankles somewhere in the vicinity of my ears. And if I wasn't so tired, I'd rub my clit again. Right now. I'd get my pussy all nice and wet, then make you watch me come."

"Fuck," he groans the curse—and to my delight, he's stiffer than semi-hard now. Because I'm truly not opposed to torturing him, and his very strong imagination can have a field day with the little I just gave him.

"Anyway," I tell him, closing my eyes. "Good night."

He groans again before laughing. "Sleep tight, Abbie girl. Because I'm going to kiss you everywhere tomorrow."

Everywhere. Anticipation fills me again, until I'm like a little girl lying in bed on Christmas Eve and hoping to hear the clippity-clop of reindeer hooves on the roof.

I fall asleep while waiting for Santa to come.

* * *

I'M NOT SURE WHAT WAKES me. It's dark, telling me the fire has died down, so at least a few hours have passed. But it's not yet freezing cold in the way it gets nearer to dawn.

And I'm not spooned anymore. I must have rolled over onto my belly. My leg still touches Reed's, but that's it.

Reed's still asleep, each breath deep and even, his body radiating luscious warmth. I scoot oh-so-slowly closer again, trying not to wake him.

Maybe I don't try hard enough. Or maybe he senses me moving, because his steely arm hooks around my middle and with a drowsily mumbled "C'mere," Reed drags me bodily up against his chest, no longer spooning but front-to-front. He nuzzles his face into my hair with a sleep-slurred, "Smell s'good."

That wakes me up a bit more, though I'm not sure about him. Once he's got me close, his hold around my waist relaxes and his breaths even out, each exhalation warming my ear and cheek.

Then, although he doesn't move, his body doesn't seem as relaxed anymore. As if tension and awareness are seeping into his extremities. His inhalations deepen.

"Reed?" It's hardly a murmur, so I won't disturb him if he *is* still asleep.

"I'm here." His quiet reply still has a bedtime thickness to it, but not a hint of drowsiness. "Do you need me to move over or let you go?"

"No, I— It's after midnight." And in case my meaning isn't clear, "So…it's tomorrow."

When he intended to kiss me. Perhaps he would have, if I'd given him the chance.

But I kiss him first. Well, *first* I launch myself at him, bowling him over onto his back, then climbing aboard. I straddle his stomach, take his face in my hands—his shaved jaw only slightly rough under my palms—*then* kiss him. Rather hungrily, in truth.

Thankfully, Reed is hungry, too.

And, oh, it's such *good* kissing. Not the rote kissing that always happens when a lip-lock is nothing but the expected first step on a path farther south. Truthfully, I assumed kissing Reed would be like that, too. I only saw the decision to kiss him as a first step toward what was inevitably next, knowing it would never *just* be a kiss. Even when I jumped him, the purpose of kissing him was mostly to get the engine started.

But now that I'm here, I could do this for *hours*. Kissing Reed is such a pleasure in itself. Stroking my tongue over his. The soft suction on my lips. The delicious wet slide of our mouths. The massaging grip of one large hand on my ass, the other curled firmly around my nape. Drawing back for air and feeling his smile beneath mine. Angling my head and going in for more.

I go in for more *so* many times. Then after—I don't know how long it's been—I finally come up for air again, resting my forehead against his, my breathing harsh and my whole body feeling hot and shivery.

Honestly, I'm a little blindsided. Again.

Straddling him as I am, I ride the rise and fall of his own quickened breaths. His fingers tighten around my nape, his thumb in the little hollow beneath my ear. I didn't know how good a thumb feels right there. How strangely comforting and yet possessively demanding, all at once.

Reed gently nips my bottom lip. "I like it when we aren't enemies."

"No," I say, "we still are."

"Dammit. Still?"

"Oh, don't grumble. I'm a complicated person. We've been enemies all our lives, you think that disappears in a poof? I've got twenty years of baggage to unload before I can clear you as a friend." I grin against his mouth, then go in for a lick across the edge of his teeth. "For tonight, though, I'll pretend you *aren't* my enemy."

"That's acceptable." He squeezes my ass then runs his hand up my back. "So what would you like your not-enemy to do to you?"

So much. But there's one *leeetle* problem. Leaning in close, I whisper hotly in his ear, "I want you to tell me that you've got condoms in your pack."

"Oh, *fuck.*" It's too dark to make out his expression, but by his tone, I have to imagine a comical portrait of abject uncertainty and horrified dismay. "Fuck. Do I?"

"Go check. You've been lucky so far this holiday."

"My luck's not running out now." Determination fills his voice and he rolls us over, then leaves me in the middle of the bed. "I'll hike to the nearest town if I have to."

The sudden glare of a halogen lantern almost blinds me. I pull a blanket up around my shoulders and sit huddled, watching as Reed grabs his pack, throws it down to the floor. He drops to his knees and begins searching through it, dragging out items and tossing them aside. No kid on Christmas morning ever put more energy into tearing away wrapping paper and ripping into a box, praying that Santa brought him the one gift he wanted more than anything else, than Reed does digging into that bag.

"I've thrown all kinds of shit in here over the years," he tells me, as if the collection of stuff accumulating around him wasn't already proof of that. We could live for weeks off the number of protein bars he carries around. "I think I tossed condoms in here at some point. And I've got no idea what might be in some of these pockets—*FUCK YES!*"

Triumphantly he emerges from the pack's uncharted depths with what used to be a black box. Now the packaging is flattened and tattered at the edges. Abruptly the triumph drains from his expression. He carries the box over to the lantern, where he squints and brings the package nearer to his face.

He casts me a grim look. "They expired a month ago. And they were out in below-freezing temps for a few days."

Oh god. Lust wars with caution. I bite my knuckle. "Is it worth it? What do you think?"

While contemplating, he turns the box over and over in his hands. Considering the tentpole in his pajama pants, I'm not surprised when he decides, "If they seem all right when we open them, I'm game. You?"

"Yes. I also have an IUD." I don't have a tentpole but I can talk myself into almost anything. Of course, birth control isn't the only concern. "Are you usually protected?"

"Always. And it's been a while. A long while," he adds with a note of chagrin.

"Nothing wrong with that. And me, too. Been a while, always protected." I blow out my cheeks. "All right, then. How many are left?"

"The full dozen. I haven't used any of them." He swiftly detours to the fireplace and tosses in more wood, then a few long strides carry him back to the side of the bed. He doesn't turn off the lantern. "How many more days will I be here?"

"Still another week." Why doesn't that seem long enough? Before, seven days stuck with Reed Knowles seemed like an eternity. "Unless the snow doesn't melt by New Year's."

He pulls the strip of condoms out of the smashed box. "Then we'll have to ration these until we're sure it's melting."

"So it'll be like the Twelve Days of Christmas, but it's twelve fucks, instead." As he tears one off, I sing, "♪On the first fuck of Christmas, my enemy gave to me...a cock in a latex sheath!♪"

My voice is as terrible as always. But he doesn't cringe, doesn't cover his ears.

Instead he laughs and leans in to kiss me, still standing beside the bed while I'm in the center of it. Pulling back, he catches my gaze and tucks a loose curl behind my ear.

"I'm going to work hard to find out what you like, but is there anything I should stay away from because it'll ruin this for you?"

I blink at him in surprise. But I guess there are a few things. "Well, if you go down on me—"

"When," he interrupts. "Not *if*. The only thing that'll stop me is if you say now you don't like it."

My heart skips a little. "*When* you do, I don't like being spit on."

"No worries there. If I can't get you wet enough, I'm doing something wrong." His hand slips under the blankets and strokes up the length of my thigh, making me shiver. "Anything else?"

"I like dirty talking but— Do you usually?" Maybe it won't even be an issue.

"I do. I can't help it, mostly. My head gets in there and just takes over." His eyes crinkle at the corners and he still hasn't taken his gaze from my face. "If you want anything specific said, at any time, just let me know. And that's where my head will go."

I'm fascinated and a little distracted by the idea of his head taking over instead of simply leaving the building while he's fucking, but I don't want to forget the important part. "Not something specific to say, but *not* say. I don't like being called a slut or whore just because I'm eager."

"All right." His thumb slides along the elastic edge of my panties. "Anything else?"

"I don't mind rough or a spank on my ass. But I don't

like my tits slapped—or my face, even if it's not a hard slap."

His expression hardens, his fingers stilling their soft caress. "Who—?" He bites off the question, his eyes closing. "No. Not now. We'll discuss that later. Anything else?"

"I can't think of anything now." I'm starting to lose the ability to think at all. "What about you? Is there anything you don't like?"

For a long second, Reed merely looks at me, his brows drawn. "No one's ever asked me that before. Hold on while I think."

He means 'hold on' literally, because he scoops me up and sits on the side of the bed with me straddling his hips—lowering me carefully, I realize, not so he doesn't crush his erection but to make sure I don't land on the bruised muscle of his thigh. He wraps a forearm around my back, as if to hold me in place.

His free hand begins undoing the buttons of my pajama shirt. "I prefer that you don't call me James while you're coming."

"Say what?"

"It happened once."

I study his face. His focus is on his fingers—and maybe on everything that he's revealing beneath my pajamas—but I can't read his expression. "Is that a sad story or a funny one?"

"Funny."

I'm glad. It's so strange, the realization that I don't want to think of Reed being hurt. Especially if he cared enough for another woman to *be* hurt. "I'll try not to forget your name, then."

"I don't think it was a matter of forgetting, but pretending she was with someone else. I suppose it's a sad story for her."

Sounds like one. "I'm not pining for anyone named James or otherwise, so we're in the clear. Any other dislikes?"

"Just one." Finished with the buttons, he cups my face, rubs his thumb over my upper lip. "Don't fake anything with me, Abbie girl. Make me work for it if you're not enjoying it."

Heart pounding, I nod. "Anything else?"

"No."

"Then I'd like you to get to work now."

"Yes, ma'am," he says and hauls me in, claiming my mouth in a kiss that's good, still *so* good, but one that seems to take everything he discovered in our kisses before and spins it into a new purpose.

I can't smile against his mouth anymore because I'm too busy hanging on, withstanding the new onslaught that is Reed's mouth. Before there was hunger and sweetness and fun but now there's fire, searing everything, stealing all of the oxygen and leaving me gasping, pulling him closer, trying to get more. My hands push into his hair—and he winces into our kiss, because I forgot. I forgot that he'd gotten whacked.

I blather a "Sorry, sorry, sorry."

"S'alright, Abbie." His lips reddened, looking somewhat dazed, he pulls back—and I'm *so* sorry then, until he lifts my breast and dips his head. Then there's fire again, drawing my nipple into the heat of his mouth, burning me straight through.

And I want more, more, more. I arch back against the iron bar of his forearm, offering him better access—and that movement rocks my center against the rigid stand of his cock. He moans around my nipple, a sound that rumbles over his tongue and injects into my blood, because the fire spreads downward and I rub again, and again, my knees digging into the bed on either side of his hips, using that leverage to ride his full length, pussy-soaked cotton against cotton pulled taut over hardened flesh, the friction over my clit so maddening but so unbearably delicious.

Groaning, he releases my nipple and presses his face into the softness of my breast. His hand grips my ass, slowing me just a little, meeting each rock of my hips with a subtle lift of his own. "It was hot as fuck when you did this the other morning. I wanted to fill you with my cock right there."

A laugh escapes through my ragged breaths. "I shouldn't have been so surprised to wake up that way. I saw your dick when you got into bed. It took me hours to stop thinking of it. But then apparently I dreamed of it."

He looks up at me, eyes narrowing. "I'll have to fix that."

"Fix what?"

"You stopped thinking of it. I'll make it so you never do again. I'll get so deep into you, you'll always be feeling it. But let's get you wet enough, first."

I'm pretty sure that I'm already wet enough, but I'd be the last person to protest when Reed flips us around, goes down to his knees and drags my ass to the edge of the

KATI WILDE

mattress. His fingers hook into my panties and he strips them off, then pushes my thighs wide.

"Christ. Look at you." His voice is deep and reverent. His hands cup my knees, holding me spread, and he bows his head to kiss the soft skin halfway up my inner thigh. "Such a sweet little cunt. I should get my fill of looking in now, before I've wrecked it."

My body's trembling too hard to laugh again, but I manage a gasping sort of snort. "Aren't *you* full of yourself?"

"You'll be full of me, too, Abbie girl." His mouth skims higher; his hand slides up my other thigh, using his elbow now to hold me open. With no hesitation, he slicks his thumb up my slit and over my clit, forcing me to bite my lip against the desperate mewling sound that I almost make. His thumb returns to my entrance and gently presses his way in. "You saw my cock. You know what you'll be trying to take into this little hole. I know I should go easy with a pussy so sweet. But I don't think I'll be holding back."

"You won't need to." I hope he doesn't even try to. "It's not my first rodeo, rough rider. And a funny thing about vaginas: they bounce back."

"Thank fuck for that. And for this sweet, resilient little pussy." Abruptly he spreads me with his fingers and dives in for a hot, swirling lick. Then another. He has to hold me down when I writhe upward, biting the back of my hand, feeling nothing but the rough and the slick of his tongue.

He pauses, looking up at me. I can almost breathe. Then a suckling kiss to my clit rips away all the air and I'm gasping, flailing.

Until he pauses again.

Testing. Or teasing. I'm not sure which, but he's murdering me.

"Reed." I pant his name.

"Hmm?" he hums, rubbing his thumb over my clit, his tongue slipping down to my entrance.

"I need to come. Please. Save the torture for round two."

And, oh god. Because it turns out that Reed eats pussy just like he kisses. As if it's the most important thing he'll ever do. As if there's nothing in the world he enjoys more. His fingers push deep and his mouth covers my clitoris, taking me over inside and out with each lick, each thrust, each time he sucks on my clit and flicks his tongue. My last surviving brain cell remembers that I can't fist my hands in his hair and rub my cunt all over his face so instead I rip at the blankets under me, making gurgling noises in my throat that probably aren't normally made by anyone living. Then Reed groans, as if he loves what he's doing to me (god help me, I love it, too), and his fingers bend and his knuckles rub in just the right spot, and he does another of those swirling kisses. I come like some crazed feral creature, clawing the blankets and wailing his name (*not* James, what an absolute fool that woman was.) When my convulsions stop, I ease back down—gasping, maybe crying a little, covering my face with my hands and trying to recover. But Reed doesn't make it easy, spreading me wide again and slowly licking me up, then placing a gentle kiss against my still-quivering belly.

"So fucking beautiful, Abbie. You taste so damn good. *If* I go down," he scoffs at the memory, then kisses higher, higher. "I'm going to do that again and again."

My head turns to the side and I notice Hot Biscuit Slim, curled up and sleeping at the end of the bed. As if the most cataclysmic orgasm in the history of humanity hadn't just taken place three feet away from him.

How could he sleep through that?

Then I forget my cat, because Reed's kisses reach my breastbone. The single brain cell I have left remembers that I *can* touch his shoulders, his chest. So I do as he rises over me, scraping my fingers through the hair covering his pecs, dragging my nails down his sides, glorying in the solidity of him, the warmth.

He kisses me slow and deep before putting his mouth to my ear. "You want to be fucked, Abbie girl? Want me to fill up the hot little cunt that I just made wet enough to take me?"

My reply is a frantic nod as I bring his mouth to mine again. And his strength is really something ridiculous, because while kissing he casually picks me up and deposits me in the center of the bed. He only draws back to shuck his pajamas—oh my, he's a show-er *and* a grow-er. Long and almost obscenely thick, more meaty than veiny.

I'm not at all upset about that.

He rips open the condom packet and carefully rolls it on. "Does it look all right?" *Please, Santa, let it be all right.*

"All good so far."

That applies to more than just the rubber. "Credit where it's due—you are exceeding yesterday's anticipation. No disappointment yet."

"Told you I'd prove you wrong." He grins when I huff, then crawls up over me, hooking my right leg over his left elbow as he goes. "You okay like this?"

"I'm flexible," I tell him breathlessly, my anticipation cranking up to high again as he settles between my thighs. My teeth dig into my bottom lip when he takes his shaft in hand and furrows the broad tip through the folds of my pussy, notching against my entrance.

"Good," he says, breath ragged. "Because I want to watch this little cunt stretch around my cock." A groan rips from him as he pushes in and slides deep, deeper. "Just like that. Look how you take me, Abbie girl. Fuck, you feel so damn good."

So good. I can't think. Can't feel anything but how full I am. It burns a little. Aches a little. It doesn't *hurt*, but I'm so acutely aware that he's inside me, the penetration is a little overwhelming.

Then a lot overwhelming, all at once. Not just how good it feels, but how *right* it feels.

It's almost terrifying.

Reed's mouth briefly finds mine before he tries to catch my eyes. "All right?"

I need him to move. I'll be all right if he moves. I'll process everything else later.

"I'm okay," I tell him, then wrap my free leg around him, digging my heel into his ass, urging him forward. "But move. Move move move. And say dirty things."

Anything to pull me out of my own head.

Slowly he withdraws, so thick that the friction against my inner walls is insane, despite how slick and aroused I am. My eyes roll back and I take a gulping breath. Then his cock pushes inside me again, and the pleasure finally bursts through the overwhelming fullness, and it's all I can do not to scream.

"You're taking me so good, Abbie girl. So hot and wet, just sucking me in." Reed grunts when he bottoms out, then angles me up higher. "You didn't imagine this, did you? When I came in through that snowstorm. You never thought your sworn enemy would have you in this bed, spreading you open so he could stuff you full of his cock."

Oh god. "I didn't."

"I'd have known right away, if my head wasn't bashed in. If I'd gotten here with my brains intact and saw you—so vibrant, so sexy—I'd have known how much you needed to be fucked."

"So much," I say, then cry out on a deep thrust.

"I know exactly how it would have been." He pulls back and begins rubbing my clit, before slowly sliding back in, making me stretch for him again. "I'd have seen you, then I'd have fallen to my knees, begging for a taste. Would you have let me suck your clit, Abbie? Would you have let me worship your cunt?"

ONLY ONE BED

I gasp out a "Maybe"—*I can't believe I might come again, I might come again*—"if you begged enough."

"For this soft little pussy? I'd have begged." His thumb slides faster, while his cock begins short, deep digs. "I'd have done anything if it meant you let me inside you. I'd have crawled across the floor to you just for the hope of getting between these pretty thighs. But I wouldn't have had any condoms that night. Would you make me stop or would you let me fill you up with my filthy cum?"

My head gets in there and just takes over. And I understand now. Because he's taking over mine, too. Painting the scene in my brain. Sharing his imagination with me so that it's like I'm being fucked twice—inside my body and inside my head.

"I'd have let you." Over and over again. "I'd have let you fill me up."

"Fuck, Abbie," he groans, pushing deep again. "You just squeezed me so tight. You like that thought—of me coming in, taking you to this bed? While you're still hating me? I'd have to be so rough with you." His thumb slicks a wet trail up from my clit, then he presses down, right above my pubic bone. I suck in a strangled breath, bucking beneath him, the pressure inside unlike anything I've ever felt before as his cock rubs back and forth, working my G-spot better than any toy ever has. "Because you'd be fighting me, wouldn't you? Fighting how much you want it. But do you want it, Abbie girl? This fat Knowles cock? Your enemy's cum?"

"Yes! Oh god oh god." I'm not fighting him but I can't

stop moving, can't stop this frantic twist of my body and thrust of my hips. "Reed!"

"I'm here, Abbie. I'm here. Let go."

His thumb slides down to my clit again and then I'm arching back, spine bowed and crying out as the orgasm barrels into me.

"That's it. Fuck, oh fuck. The way you come around my cock." The deep reverence in his voice is becoming strained by tension, his shaft still rhythmically fucking into me, his words slowly piercing my euphoric haze. "You're so beautiful and so tight. I can't hold back. But do you need me to hold back? Abbie girl, do you need longer? Need to come again?"

"Reed." Fiercely I take hold of his face between my hands and draw his mouth to mine. "You worked so hard for this. And you promised to wreck it."

"Oh thank fuck," he heaves out on a laugh. Roughly he kisses me, then reaches up to grab the headboard, shoving forward until I'm almost folded in half with my knees pressed into my shoulders, his thrusts as hard and erratic as his words. "Like it was made for me. So goddamn tight. This sweet cunt. So perfect. Abbie. I—"

His mouth crushes mine, but he only groans against my lips, not kissing. His thick shaft spasms within me, and I can't help but squeeze my inner muscles to intensify the sensation. Aside from my own orgasm, this is my very favorite part of sex. That moment when he loses all control. Of knowing that it's all for me—and Reed is giving more and longer than any before. He pushes against me again, as if trying to get deeper as he comes.

"Just like that, Knowles." My voice is a purr. "I'm such a bad girl, being so mean to you, calling you my enemy. But now you've fucked me and filled up my pussy with all your hot cum." Another twitch of his heavy flesh inside me. I rock beneath him, my inner walls clutching him tight. "And you made me love it, Reed. You made me love the way you fucked me and now I love the feel of your big cock coming so, *so* deep inside me."

His hips jerk again. Then with a final agonized grunt, his rigid body seems to collapse over me—though he's still gripping the headboard and doesn't crush my body beneath his. With a satisfied smile, I wrap my legs around his waist. Not letting him go yet. Even softening, he feels so good inside me, and I love that heavy full feeling.

"Fuck." Between heaving breaths, he kisses me and says again, "Fuck. You're amazing."

"You're all right, too." I pat his sweaty chest. "You did a good job."

He laughs then hangs his head. "I'd love to stay inside you like this, but I need toss the rubber."

"Then we'll meet back here, because a UTI while we're snowbound is not my idea of a good time."

He gives a grunt of agreement and carefully withdraws. I hie off to the bathroom, pee and clean up. By the time I'm back out, he's got the lantern off, his pajama pants on, and the covers smoothed out again. The bed's missing a grumpy orange cat.

"Hot Biscuit Slim?"

"Probably hiding underneath," Reed says. "I felt him take off when the bed started thumping."

"What a 'fraidy cat. Any breaks in the condom?" As hot as it is to think of his cum filling me up, I'm not quite ready for the reality of it.

I'm not quite ready to consider a lot of what happened inside me tonight.

"All good. Unless the latex broke down at a microscopic level and we're both diseased."

"You really are good at coming up with horrifying scenarios," I say. Reed only grins while he absently scratches his hairy chest, and I know I'll keep talking myself into this without any effort at all. "I guess we'll continue taking that risk, though. Eleven more times. We'll say that we're testing post-expiration condom integrity."

He turns down the covers and climbs in after me. "So we're fucking in the name of science?"

"Of course. And we can send the results to my mom later. 'Hey, here's my science fair project from when I was out at Harris's cabin. Aren't you proud of me?'"

First we're laughing, then kissing, then I'm sighing happily while he pulls me back to spoon with him again. I close my eyes—and remember the most important thing about yesterday becoming tomorrow.

"Reed?"

"Hmm?"

"Merry Christmas."

He holds me tighter. "Merry Christmas, Abbie girl."

Reed

WHAT THE HELL HAS THIS WOMAN DONE TO ME?

I watch Abbie sleeping, her expression soft, her cheek snuggled into her pillow—and she's lying on her belly about a foot away. She went to sleep in my arms but she's not there now. Maybe she got too hot, maybe she rolled away for some other reason. But I can count on zero fingers the number of times I've waited for a woman to begin stirring so that I can pull her close again.

Pull her close for another round, sure. But we did that about an hour ago. I woke in the dark, found Abbie on her stomach, got up behind her and hauled her onto her knees. It's usually my favorite position to fuck, not just for the depth but also the view—yet with Abbie, rutting wasn't enough. I had to turn her around so I could watch her bliss out, so I could kiss her as I came.

Then I wrapped my arms around her and we fell asleep.

Now she's slipped out of my hold again. The distance does twisty, messy things inside my chest that I know damn well isn't really about the twelve-inch gap between us. It hasn't been since the first time I held her.

Fuck, was that only yesterday? With me utterly furious when she started blaming the Knowles for ruining her Christmas. Thinking that I hadn't been wrong about the Walkers after all, because she was throwing shit at anyone that she could. Then a snowball smashed into my face, and I actually started listening to what she was screaming.

And then…and then…

I've been lucky these past days. No doubt of it. But if I have any luck left to spend throughout my lifetime, I will never again have to watch Abbie Walker's heart and soul shatter like they did when she broke down over the thought of returning to the festering hellhole she calls a home.

I don't think I'd survive seeing it again.

That was my first time holding her. I haven't gotten enough of holding her since. I haven't stopped reeling since, either. Not with the way she bounced back, even though I dealt her blow after blow. Not after I saw how vulnerable she was—but I saw her strength, too. How she'd persevered through everything that was thrown at her. Not unharmed. But persisting…and somehow doing it with good humor and cheer.

I can't begin to describe how appealing that is to me. That resilience. How she makes me laugh without trying. How she lights up everything with just her eyes.

It's adorable. And terrifying.

Yet, for me, admiring resilience like hers is nothing new. So she's done something else to me. I don't know what it is, but it's something that makes me want to hold her...and keep on holding her. As if there's a person within me who wasn't there before. A Reed Knowles who's a stranger, a man that Abbie somehow brought to life inside me.

And that...could be an idea for a book. Though I'd write a much darker version of what I suspect is happening here.

Which is also really fucking scary. Mostly because I have no idea what to do with this strange Reed Knowles growing within.

Except hold onto her as tight as I can.

ABOUT FIFTEEN MINUTES LATER, ABBIE sighs and turns her head against her pillow. Good enough. I snag her around the waist and drag her in close, face to face.

She smiles and cuddles in. "This is nice," she says sleepily.

I drop a kiss to her forehead and breathe in the scent of her hair. "Yeah, it is."

Abruptly she stiffens, her leg jerking. Goddamn cat. I *just* got her in my arms again.

"I'll take care of him," I tell her. "Stay where it's warm. How much cat food?"

"One scoop. Oh, and check the water dish. Yesterday there was ice on top. Thank you."

I do both, then rebuild the fire so the cabin can heat up a bit before we leave the bed. Sliding in next to her, I drag her close again—making sure I can see her face, brushing back the curls that escaped from her braids during our two rounds of fucking.

She catches my wrist as I draw my hand back. "Is that where I bit you?"

My scar. "You remember doing it?"

"I could hardly forget."

"I have. Mostly. Do you remember what brought it on?"

"I do." She chews on the bottom corner of her lip, her eyes searching my face. "You really want to hear?"

"Yeah," I say, though the way she's looking at me makes me wonder if I do.

She sighs reluctantly. "My mom had an appointment to see the funeral director—and we were supposed to bring anything we wanted to go into my dad's coffin. I'd made a drawing of our family. And maybe it was just really bad luck that your mom's funeral was ending as we were going in but—"

"They started shouting at each other," I say, because I do remember this part.

Solemnly she nods. "And while they were going at it, you snatched the drawing out of my hands, said it was a stupid picture and ugly as shit, then ripped it in half."

Shame fills my chest like a ball of hot lead. "I did?"

"You did." Her hand comes up to cup my cheek. "It doesn't matter."

"It does." No fucking wonder she doesn't want me to look at her painting. "I'm so damn sorry."

"You don't have to be. You were a kid. I was a kid. It doesn't matter."

It's hard to believe it doesn't really matter when her memory of me doing that horrible shit to her is still so clear. Especially since what I said was echoed later by her own family.

Just as my memory of the incident was reinforced by my father. "I mostly only remember what my dad told me happened. I'm not surprised he didn't mention that I was a nasty little bastard and had my own cruel part in it."

She nods, and her hand slips down to curl gently at the side of my neck. "Did he ever let you be? Ever let you *not* be angry, and just quietly grieve?"

"No. And since you're asking, I guess your mom didn't let you, either?"

"She told us, flat-out *told* us, that our dad was dead and it was the Knowles's fault. Did your dad say something similar?"

"Every goddamn day."

"That's why I truly mean that it doesn't matter. Because we were kids." Her thumb traces the line of my jaw, rasping over my morning stubble, and it takes everything in me not to capture her hand and kiss her palm like some besotted swain. "I'm pretty sure my mom knew what she was doing, arriving earlier than our appointment, then waiting where your dad would see her. I'm not sure either of us can be blamed for following where our parents were leading us or for believing what they told us. So neither one of us is at fault, not really. Not for what you said. Not for me biting you." Her lips quirk and her eyes crinkle. "Of course, if either of us did the same now…I'm not sure we'd have an excuse."

If she's trying to lighten the load that we're carrying, then I'll help her. "There's a bite mark on my shoulder that says you haven't changed too much. Though you didn't draw blood, at least."

She grins up at me. "I came like some kind of wild animal. I'm surprised your dick wasn't crushed."

"If you hadn't made my dick so damn hard, it probably would've been." Not that I'm complaining. And I'm looking forward to it again, that tight fluttering squeeze down the full length of my cock.

I'm stiffening now just thinking of it.

Her head tilts. "If you don't mind saying…why are you not with your dad? Because it *is* Christmas. Is it just that he's an asshole?"

That deflates my burgeoning erection. "Partially. I don't talk to him much. We haven't done Christmas together for years. Nothing beyond a text, sometimes not even that. I do see him now and again. We know enough of the same people that we cross paths. But I've just got nothing to say to him."

She gives me a knowing look. "Does he have anything to say to you?"

"Heh. Nothing worth hearing. He boasts about what he buys—his toys, he always calls them—and his big plans and his money. It's always a whole lot of posturing, even when it's just him and me. His own son. He doesn't need to prove anything to me but it's always the same shit. And we're just completely fucking different. No common interests, nothing worth sharing with him. And he's so goddamn loud. Always talking over everyone. Railroading over anyone else's opinions."

"Ah," she says softly.

"What?"

"That's why you said I was silenced. I didn't know how to put it, the way I felt with Lauryn. But you did. Because being silenced isn't unfamiliar to you."

I shake my head—not in denial, but in surprise that she'd made the connection so quickly. It took me twenty-one years and about a hundred and fifty thousand words before I understood what he does. "It's not the same—it's not negativity—but I sure as hell wasn't allowed to have an opinion that didn't match his. So I learned to keep my mouth shut. But that was normal, growing up. Or I thought it was. 'A good son respects his father's authority.' I can't tell you how many times I heard that."

Her eyes narrow. "A good son respect his father's authority or respects his father?"

"Pretty sure he thought they were the same thing."

"But you don't," she says.

"I'd say a good father is one that his son *can* respect."

She smiles as if she likes that answer. "Did the respect ever go both ways?"

"Seemed like it did following the shouting match I told you about. As if he recognized me as my own man after."

"'Seemed?'"

This woman never misses a thing. "We'd cross paths, he'd slap my back and ask if I was doing all right, ask if I was getting enough pussy, and remind me that I should come to him if I needed any help with my business. That's his version of respect."

Her nose wrinkles. "How fun."

"Easy to shrug off, at least. Though I bet if I ever openly disagreed with him, I'd get the 'good son' speech again. It wasn't until the thing with your mom's house that I realized I actively disliked him. And that I couldn't respect him."

She comes up on her elbow, eyes wide. "Really?"

"It was his gloating." How do I begin to explain this? "After she died, his rage against your family was always on my mother's behalf. Because of the lawsuits and the way your mom trashed her name every time she could. I can't say I felt much different. Even after accepting that what my mom did was unethical, it was still real fucking hard to see her name ground into the dirt. So I always respected my father for how fiercely he protected her good name. She'd cheated on him, yet he still protected her. I admired him for that loyalty, that dedication."

"I understand that," she says softly. "She was still his wife and he was defending her. The same way my mother defended my father. They each just…ignored the shitty cheating parts and clung to what was good."

"Yeah, well—it took me a while to realize that it was never about defending her. The lawsuits were over with, your mom is easy to block on social media—"

"What? Why? No! Oh god." Her eyes close and her face glows pink. "Did she leave reviews on your business page?"

"Yeah." And her blush is damn cute. "Or she'd reply to people posting on my pages and tell them not to trust the results of my inspections, because I could be bribed."

Her face goes a brighter red. And though it's adorable, the depth of her embarrassment is also painful to see.

"It's all right," I assure her. "It was irritating now and then—I'm pretty sure that shit I said to Harris was shortly after I had to delete another of those comments—but it's nothing at this point. I'm done with all the Hatfield and McCoy shit. I wasn't lying when I said that I didn't think of the Walkers much at all anymore."

"For a long time, I didn't think of the Knowles much, either. Aside from when Harris mentioned you, but that was just—" She shrugs, as if to show how nothing it was. "Until they moved in and my mom told me…well, all the shit she told me. Then I despised you again."

Because she's spent the last eighteen months dealing with the fallout. "I won't pretend I didn't get some satisfaction out of seeing Angela Walker come to him for help, not after all the shit she said and did over the years—or that I didn't feel there was some poetic justice in her not having the cash to pay off the county because she'd spent it on all those lawsuits. But his gloating left a real bad taste in my mouth. Partially because gloating when you've so clearly won is just shitty behavior—"

"This, coming from a man who shouted 'fuck yes' when I finally laughed."

I grin, because I'm still feeling good about that. "Spontaneous celebrations are exempt."

"If you say so." But she looks as if she's close to laughing again. "I interrupted you. Go on. You were saying his gloating was shitty."

"That was part of it. The rest was because he always went on about defending my mother. Protecting her name. But while he was gloating, every fucking word out of his mouth was about destroying everything your father once owned, everything he'd cared about. That's what was getting him off. I realized then, there was no loyalty to my mother. For almost twenty years, he'd hated your father, but it wasn't because your dad stole my mom from him. It wasn't because your dad ruined his marriage or his happiness or broke his heart. Your dad stole his pride, and my father couldn't fucking deal with that."

"Oh," she says softly. "You think he felt emasculated when she ran off with my dad?"

"Yeah. So when that man's wife came asking him for help, he razed everything that man ever had to the ground and finally proved he had the bigger dick. And as unbearable as he was to be around before, he was worse after. Then he married Karilee."

That detour catches her off-guard. She stares at me for a long second before venturing, "Are you...upset that he replaced your mother?"

"Not at all. Like I said, we aren't around each other much—even during the holidays. But he remarried this year and I felt...obligated." There's no other way to put it. "He's got a lodge not far from here. They wanted to make a Christmas get-together a new family tradition, so they invited me and Karilee's parents—and her brothers and sister. All teenagers and absolute shits."

"Her siblings are teenagers?" She looks at me in horror. "Is Karilee that young, too?"

"She can legally drink, but yeah. He needed his ego stroked, I guess."

"Pretty sure she's not just stroking his ego." She studies me. "I understand the obligation to go, though. Did you fight with him and that's why you left?"

I wish. "Karilee tried to join me in the shower."

"No!" Abbie jackknifes up to sitting, jaw dropped open. "Your new stepmother!? Tell me you're joking."

"Not a bit. She came prancing in, bare ass naked, and slid open the shower door."

"What did you do?" She covers her mouth with her steepled hands, her eyes alight. "I'm sorry but this is the most amazingly horrible thing I've ever heard! It's like a soap opera! What did you do?"

"Grabbed a towel and got the fuck out of there."

"Did she say anything when she opened the shower?"

"'Oops!' But like this." I thrust out my chest and flutter my eyelashes. "'Oops!'"

Abbie doubles over, clutching helplessly at my shoulder as

177

she laughs. "I-I'm s-sorry," she manages after a minute, wiping her eyes. "It m-must have been tra-traumati-traumatizing."

"No, I was just pissed. I packed up my shit, texted Harris and told my dad's housekeeper I was taking his snowmobile—because even with 4-wheel drive, I didn't trust my truck to get through the snow at that point. Didn't say a damn word to anyone else. I just left."

"Your *dad's* snowmobile?" she echoes delightedly. "Did you wreck one of his toys?"

"I did. I'm not a bit sorry, either." For a whole lot of reasons, but—"Mostly because coming here might be the best thing that ever happened to me."

For the barest second, her eyes widen and she sucks in a breath. Then she laughs. "Not if we'll both need antibiotics after using those condoms. It won't be the best thing then."

It was too much of a confession. And it came too fast. Because I'm getting to know Abbie Walker. I'm beginning to understand how some of her jokes are a deflection. Not all of them. Not even most of them. But when she doesn't know what to think or how to feel.

And although I don't fully understand what's going on inside me—who this stranger is living in me now—I have no intention of hiding how much I like her. She's been too fucking unappreciated by the people closest to her. So I'm not going to deal her measly little portions of praise. She's going to know how amazing I think she is. And maybe there will come a day when her instinct isn't to defend herself, and she can accept such a confession for what it is.

Or whatever it turns out to be.

Until then, I've got plenty of ways to appreciate Abbie Walker. "You're worth the risk," I tell her, then capture her lips. She gasps into my mouth before melting against me, her arms wreathing my neck. I take advantage of that boneless acquiescence to maneuver her onto the center of the bed, where I stretch out alongside her for a leisurely kiss and not-so-leisurely roaming of my hand.

Her tits are magnificent, her nipples a pretty pink when they're soft and a darker rose after they've been pinched and teased. Her navel's a sweet little outie, and a single spot next to her ribs is ticklish enough that the brush of my fingers makes her squirm and laugh into our kiss. Her auburn bush is neatly trimmed into a landing strip—though I wonder if it was before yesterday. She might keep it tidy for herself, but I also might not be the only one who shaved. I'll need to do it again soon. I ought to do it now. Her chin is already reddened from my stubble. My razor twice a day, from now on.

That sounds like a good schedule for eating her pussy, too.

She's about ready for my mouth. My fingers slip down between her clenched thighs, where her pussy's already dripping. She moans a broken stutter into our kiss when I begin playing with her clit, circling and teasing, my fingertips so wet they might as well be a tongue.

"Your choice, Abbie girl," I tell her, my voice roughened by hunger. "You want my mouth kissing you up here or down there? I'll make you come either way."

Her face screws into a grimace, as if I've asked her to make the most difficult decision of her life. She's locked in that monumental internal struggle for ten endless seconds before she finally bursts out with, "Down!" Though once decided, she fully commits, shoving at my shoulders, helping me on my way.

I'm grinning so hard while holding in a laugh that at first I can't do anything except rub my face against her cunt, coating my lips and chin with her wetness and her scent. One look up the length of her torso makes my hunger come roaring back again. Because she's watching me with heavy-lidded eyes, half-propped against the pillow with one arm cocked behind her head. Her hair's a messy tumble over her shoulders, the tips teasing her nipples. She's got her teeth pinching her bottom lip, making that upper lip—already swollen from my kisses—look so pouty that I feel a desperate need to make her come so that I can go back up and kiss it again.

So I hook her legs over my shoulders and dive in, adoring her taste, adoring every sound she makes, adoring the way she loses herself as she gets closer and closer. I'm forced to hold her down when her wild gyrations reach their peak—and when she comes, shaking and crying my name, there's nothing in this world more delicious than the pulse of her cunt on my tongue.

Her hands are covering her face when I head back up, as if she needs another second to recover. I kiss her nipple, which is about as pouty and as rosy as her lip. When she finally peeks at me, I tell her, "Your thighs are the best Christmas gift I've ever opened."

She laughs, and when I get to her mouth she's still smiling. "Since I'm the one who came, isn't it my gift?"

"Making you come all over my tongue is my gift to myself." Just as this kiss is. Her mouth softens under mine, and I take a long slow taste. But I should have known better than to let my guard down.

Abbie reaches down and strokes her soft hands the length of my aching cock. "So making you come all over my tongue will be *my* gift to myself."

"No." My voice sounds hoarse, but only because I'm locked in a battle against the need to fuck myself into her grip like a mindless brute. But I don't fight anything else, rolling onto my back to let her do as she likes to me. "This'll be my present, too."

"So greedy," she says, kissing her way down my chest. "You get all the presents?"

"Yeah. Because I'm bigger than you."

She presses her face into my abdomen and laughs. "What does that have to do with anything?"

"I don't know. Honestly, my brain is short-circuiting."

"What could possibly be distracting you?" she asks, then licks the underside of my shaft from balls to tip. "Are you thinking of how this monster felt when you shoved it inside me?"

I was only thinking of her tongue and how I'm not going to last even two minutes—but now I'm thinking of being inside her, too. So I'll probably last only one minute.

"But there will be no getting into me yet." She gives the head an open-mouthed suckling kiss, coaxing a drop of pre-cum from the slit with her tongue, just about killing me. "We've already used two condoms and we're only at the beginning of the first day."

"I can't count to two right now, Abbie girl," I groan. "Unless you count my two balls that will explode before you begin sucking, the way you're teasing me."

"I'm just pointing out that it'll be easier to ration if we use our mouths and hands more often."

"Is that what's happening? Rationing?"

Abbie's answer is to ruthlessly use both her mouth and her hands for a glorious five minutes, then swallow every drop when I come. I'm near delirious as I reach for her—but she's already on her way back up, snuggling in against my side, letting me hold her tight.

I wasn't fully joking when I'd said both were my presents. But I hadn't realized how true it was. Every second with Abbie seems like a gift. Every touch. Every word.

That's never happened before. I've dated but have never been in a relationship that went beyond casual. I've sure as hell never before wanted to spend time with someone like I want to with Abbie.

The same is even true of my friends. I enjoy spending time with them—Harris, a few others—but I never feel like I'm missing out on anything when they're not around. I get along by myself too well, and it's always a bit of a relief after being out with them when I'm on my own again.

Yet I feel like I might miss out when I'm not with Abbie. Her every word. Her every expression. I want to hear and see them all. And I might wonder what the hell she has done *to* me, but I'm beginning to suspect that the real question is—

What the hell am I going to do when she's done *with* me?

Because Abbie might be done the second this vacation is over. She joked about remaining enemies because she can't so easily discard so much baggage, but it's no joke that she's got twenty years of shit to work through, plus all that she recently discovered about her mom lying to her. And being isolated here with me will be a lot different than being with me back in the city, where her mom and sister will rip her to shreds simply for associating with me, let alone allowing me to stick my cock inside her. So when Abbie leaves here, it'll be a hell of a lot easier for her to just tell me we're done—tell me that I'm nothing more than a holiday fling—than deal with the very real shit that will inevitably come from our being friends. Or more than friends.

And I wouldn't blame her. Hell, I don't *want* her to bear the shit that would come her way. Not after everything she's already had to take.

And yet…I'm not giving this up. Not giving *her* up. Even if I don't know yet what it is that's making me hold onto her so tight. I'll do anything necessary so that she won't end this. So that being done with me will be harder than bearing whatever comes next.

I just wish I had a single clue about how to make her desperate to hold onto me, too.

Abbie

After we haul ourselves out of bed, I spend most of the morning lazing in front of the fire while Reed works at the table. When I finally spur myself into starting our Christmas dinner, he's right there helping. Then he helps with the cleanup after.

Now, with dishes done and my belly full, I'm lazing in front of the fire again, reading on my phone but thinking about taking a nap. Reed's in the other armchair, eyes closed—a napping overachiever.

At least, that's what I assume he's doing, until he suddenly says, "I'm begging for mercy, Abbie. I've wracked my brains but I've come up with nothing. Where the hell did you get a name like Hot Biscuit Slim?"

Oh. I didn't tell him before, simply because I didn't want to expose any part of myself that could be vulnerable. Yet now I don't hesitate before telling him, "It's kind of a two part answer, but with the same overall source. When I was little, we had a fluffy white cat that Lauryn and I named Cream Puff Fatty. After my dad…well, Mom never let us get another. So I swore that when I got my own house, I'd get a cat and name him Hot Biscuit Slim."

"Then you got your house and your cat."

"Yes."

He gives me one of his searching looks. "When you escaped from home the first time, why didn't you end up on the other side of the country? As desperate as you were to go, it doesn't seem like you went far."

"The first reason is that in-state tuition was cheaper. Plus I like this area—not far from the mountains, not far from the beach. And I did get over to the other side of the city. The cheaper side," I say, laughing. "That was far enough until they moved in. But you didn't go far, either?"

"Yeah, that was some good old nepotism at work—though at the beginning I told myself it wasn't. But the Knowles name sure didn't hurt when I was fresh out of college and hired on with the county inspecting new construction. Then when I struck out on my own, it was smarter not to start over somewhere else. I had contacts already through the county job—and from growing up as Knowles's kid."

I can't mistake the faint note of self-derision in his voice. "Do you feel like you haven't earned what you've gotten because of that?"

"Don't know. I've earned some of it. Though the name sure made it easier."

"I know how that goes. I used my father's money to buy my house. Harris pays well but I couldn't have afforded one without it. Not yet."

Somehow Reed hears what I didn't say, not even yesterday. "And that makes it even harder—with your mom and sister?"

Silently I nod.

I feel his gaze on me for a long moment. Then he says, "So you got your house and Hot Biscuit Slim. But where did you get that name?"

"My dad used to read real stories from American history to Lauryn and me before bed. Paul Bunyan was our favorite. Cream Puff Fatty and Hot Biscuit Slim were the cooks at his logging camp."

"Paul Bunyan, the lumberjack? With the blue ox?"

"Babe. Yes."

His brows arch. "These were real stories from American history?"

"Mmm-hmm. So we learned how he created the Mississippi by dragging his axe behind him when he got tired."

"Because that's always how rivers are made."

"Then there was the great popcorn blizzard. Because his men were starving, so he walked down to Kansas and bought a giant sack of corn, but on his way back the sun was so hot it all started to pop. I think of that every time it snows—or make a popcorn string." I gesture to the garland over the fireplace.

"Your poker face is fucking incredible. Though now I'm wondering if your 'I only read non-fiction' is another tall tale."

"It's true, though. There are just so many amazing things to learn—about the world, about people." It's not that I *dislike* fiction. I just don't feel like I have time for it all before I die, so I had to choose. "And there's plenty of the same stuff in it. Romance, tragedy. Horror."

His mouth quirks in a half smile. "Real life offers plenty of inspiration, for sure."

I eye him curiously. "Why horror, though?"

Reed shrugs and stretches his legs out, settling deeper into his chair. "It's just one of the things I've always enjoyed reading. Not the gore, necessarily, but the monsters and the weird shit. And the way people are so resilient despite their fear and pain. Despite everything they go through, they fight and persevere."

"So you don't write the ones where everyone ends up dying?"

"No. Not everyone lives, though. I can't say mine always end happily."

"Because they're traumatized by what they've gone through?"

"Yeah." His gaze holds mine. "But they get through. And that's the point."

I like that a lot. "How did you get started?"

"Looking for easy credits. Word around campus was that one of the tenured English professors gave As to anyone who showed up and put in the work, even if the work was half-assed. His creative writing class fulfilled a requirement, so Harris and I both took it...and it turned out I liked doing it. I was working on my stories even when I'd already completed the assignments. And I just kept on. Even after I was done with school, I'd write when I wasn't working. I had five novels finished when I finally decided to try sending one in."

"And now you have deadlines. Is that why you became an independent contractor, so you can make your own schedule?"

"Yeah. And these weeks—end of December, first of January—are always slow in real estate anyway, so I keep them free to get a good head start on a draft. The rest of the year, I try to schedule my inspections from Monday through Thursday, and spend the weekends writing."

"You must be pretty good if you got published."

His grin flashes. "I suppose that's a matter of taste. But I think they're enjoyable—and I think I get better the more I write."

"Do you ever think of writing full time?"

"Heh, no. I like to eat. And I'm financially comfortable but I wouldn't be if I only depended on royalties. There's not a lot of money in pulp horror."

"It seems like there could be?"

"Maybe, if one of the books was made into a movie or something. But that's out of my hands."

"The marketing is in your hands."

He shrugs. "My publisher doesn't spend much promoting them and I don't care to spend the time."

"Maybe I can help with that," I tell him, and the surprised glance Reed gives me probably mirrors my own surprise at having made the offer. Because if I help him, that means continuing…this. Whatever it is we have. And I haven't let myself ponder anything beyond this cabin—mostly because that'll force me to make decisions regarding my mom. Yet my chest aches when I think this upcoming week is all the time I'll have with him.

Slowly he nods. "Maybe you can."

Not holding me to anything. Probably realizing that I truly meant the offer, but that I don't know what the future has in store. Or whether he'll have any part in it. Maybe he won't *want* any part of it. Or maybe I won't want *him* to be part of it.

My heart pounds. "Can I trust you?"

"You can," he replies. Dead serious.

Oh god. Why am I about to share this with him? But I don't stop myself. Instead I get up and gesture for him to follow. Not far. Just a few steps, babbling the entire way.

"You're going to look at this and think, 'She didn't even do most of that.' It started with this silly challenge that I saw online. You take thrift store art and add something to the canvas, but the whole point was to match the style and colors. So I picked up an Impressionist seascape and decided to add a kraken attacking a ship—which ended up being a lot harder than I thought, because with the fantasy element, you need detail so your brain can interpret what it is. So I ended up with a blob—but I really liked the whole exercise of it, and began picking canvases with a more realistic style. Anyway. This is the one I'm working on now."

Reed steps closer to the easel. "So this was a finished painting, and you're altering it—but in a way that looks as if it was always meant to be part of the original artwork?"

"Yeah."

He begins examining it, and I cross my arms over my chest to stop the nervous shaking of my hands. Praying he won't think it's stupid. Or that he'll at least understand why I find it so fun.

My mom and Lauryn never did. And deep down, that might be another reason I'm out here this Christmas. Because it's impossible to buy them anything as a gift. My mom hates the commercialism and Lauryn hates everything else. But to *make* something? Even Lauryn can't nitpick recycled thrift store art. So, two years ago, I gave them each a painting.

Remembering their reactions still hurts. Even now.

My mom's was a pretty still life with florals and fruit. Not a particularly exciting subject, but incredibly detailed, almost photorealistic. So I added tiny, photorealistic ants swarming all over the still life with their own paintbrushes and palettes, making it appear that they were creating the scene they were living in—as if only something so tiny could render those minute details. And there was so *much* detail, and all of it so small—overall, it took more time than I'd ever spent on any one painting.

Mom never looked close enough to see the ants. She just thanked me, told me it was lovely—I don't think she paid attention or understood when I said the still life wasn't actually my work—then reminded me that I didn't *have* to give her anything for Christmas, and I really shouldn't.

For Lauryn's, I'd chosen a mountain landscape with a lake and added a camping scene. But the tent was wrecked, and Bigfoot reclined on a bearskin rug in front of the campfire, Burt Reynolds style, with a human femur between his teeth instead of a cigar—because when I was eight or nine, Lauryn and I ran across a picture of that old centerfold, and we decided men were gross, hairy men were even more gross (obviously I've reconsidered), and then laughed ourselves silly. But either she didn't recognize the similarity to that old photo, or she didn't remember how we laughed—or if she *did* remember, it wasn't the bright spot in her memory that it was for me.

Lauryn thanked me but added that she wasn't sure where to put it, because it didn't match the colors in her room.

Neither of the paintings is at my house now. They might be packed away in storage, but I doubt it. Before moving, they sold everything they didn't want. So I assume the paintings were sold, too.

Reed steps back, tilting his head, narrowing his eyes—which makes me realize that he still might not be focusing at one hundred percent.

"Do you need me to tell you what to look for?" Unlike the Bigfoot painting, where the change is unmistakable, this one is more on scale with the ants. The original was of a farmhouse and field in autumn golds. A peaceful, bucolic scene, with the world settling in to the restful warmth before the oncoming winter. But now the back corner of the porch is smashed and a man is peeking out from the cellar.

"I think I've got it." He gestures to the porch, the cellar, then the fields. "Are these giant footprints?"

Biting my lip, I nod. "It was originally called 'After the Harvest.' Now it's 'After the Kaiju.' I'll be adding the tip of a giant tail here, going off the canvas. Because it's gone, it's passed through. The damage is done."

"And that farmer in the cellar got lucky."

"Very lucky."

He spends another quiet minute looking, then abruptly straightens. "Wait a second. I *have* two of these. Or like these."

"Of mine?" I sell them, but the orders are made online and I package them up myself. I'd have noticed if I shipped out a canvas to a Reed Knowles.

"I suppose they must be yours. They're not the same style but— They're from the house. Before it was razed."

"What? How?"

"I was there." He closes his eyes and pinches the bridge of his nose, as if examining the painting so closely made his head ache. "I wasn't going to be. Not after the gloating. But the day of, he called me up, said he was running the bulldozer himself, and asked if I wanted to take down half of the house. And he sounded drunk, so I was just, 'Ah, fuck.'"

"You had to go save him from himself?"

"Or save everyone else. Usually in a demolition, all the utilities are disconnected and inspected before the go-ahead. But he got the permit so fast—and if he was drunk off his ass, who knew how much shit he could damage. So

I told him to wait for me. I got there and made sure the electricity was cut, that the sewage and water and gas lines were all capped—thankfully it *had* all been done. Then I asked if he'd finished the walk-through, because even after a house is abandoned, you can still end up with people in there. Sometimes the owners refusing to leave, more often a squatter. But he said if a Walker was still in there, all the better. So I did the walk-through, saw those paintings in the garage, and thought the Walkers had no taste at all." At my sucked-in breath, his head whips around. "Shit, no! Abbie. No taste for leaving them behind! Because they were clever and funny and right up my alley. But I had no idea there was an original painting that was altered. I just put it together now after seeing this one. Anyway, I took them home. Bigfoot is over my fireplace, and the ants are in my kitchen."

My heart leaping, I grab hold of his shirt and pull him in close for a hard, quick kiss. "I am going to fuck you silly, Reed Knowles."

I drag Reed to the bed (though it doesn't require much dragging). Though my intention is to fuck *him*, about ten minutes later, I've somehow ended up with his face between my legs and his fingers pumping deep, and I'm about one lick away from coming.

"Grab that condom for me, Abbie girl." His voice is rough, his thumb taking over for his tongue and rubbing, rubbing. "As soon as you come, I'm gonna be inside you again."

I fumble for the packet beside my head. Rubber number

three. I tear it open and sing, "♪On the third fuck of Christmas, my enemy gave to me: Three fingers in, two loads of cum, and a cock in a latex sheath!♪"

Reed sputters with laughter against my pussy. Just like I hoped. I take advantage of his distraction to push and pull and twist us around until he's on his back, where I roll the condom down his thick length and swing my leg over his hips.

"Abbie," he groans as I take him in. "It gets better every damn time."

Every time. I sink down, feeling that luscious stretch, the almost-*too*-deep feeling of his cock as I seat him fully inside. His jaw clenches, air hissing through his teeth, then he grips my thighs and bucks beneath me.

Lights burst behind my eyes. I fall forward, bracing my hands on his chest, shaking my head.

"Stay still, Reed. Stay still. Be good for me, and let me fuck you slow and deep." Because I remember that first time. How he asked if I needed to come again, though he was on the edge of coming himself. That memory has occupied my brain ever since. Wondering what would've happened if I'd told him to hold off until I came again. If he would have. If he *could* have. "But don't come until I'm done."

"Anything," he promises gruffly, fisting his hands in the blankets. "Anything you need."

I begin riding him slowly, my fingers stroking my clit. By the first time I come, my cunt's so slippery and swollen that each up and down slide must feel like an endless wet sucking the length of his cock. As I come the second time, Reed's heaving beneath me, his voice hoarse and begging—until I tell him it's finally his turn, and he flips me around, but doesn't stop fucking me until somehow I come again.

A while later, I'm lying bonelessly atop him and wallowing in the feel of his skin, his heat, his strength. My nap's long overdue, but I'm not sure now that I want to miss a single second of this day.

Because this truly *is* the best Christmas ever.

Reed

THIS IS THE SHITTIEST BOOK I'VE EVER WRITTEN. JUST stupid. Only one day ago, I told Abbie, *I think I get better the more I write.* Then I produce this fucking pile of garbage.

I power down the Neo and shove away from the table. Outside the window, icicle spears drip from the eaves. The sun's a blinding glare against all the white. Even as I watch, glops of snow fall from the trees. The warm front must have arrived, exactly as forecasted. Melting everything. And if it keeps up for a few more days, the roads will be clear enough for Abbie to drop me off back at my dad's lodge.

Fucking hell.

I stalk across the cabin. Abbie's at her easel, working. I *should* be working. But there's no goddamn point. The book is shit, my writing is shit, the characters are shit, the whole idea is shit. Fuck it all.

I pace back to the window. My thigh muscle pulls with

every step, though it's not as painful as before. More like the soreness that shows up two days after a brutal workout. I could use an hour in the gym now. I get some of my best thinking done in between sets, when I can let my subconscious poke and poke at the story. But pushups might do.

There's enough room by the table. I drop, do fifty, then lie on the floor. Then fifty more.

I'm about to sprawl out on the floor again when Abbie waves her hand in front of my face. She's crouching beside me, her eyes dark with concern.

I slide my headphones down.

"Are you okay?" She looks me up and down. "Is this cabin fever? Do you want to go on a hike before it gets too slushy?"

"It's not cabin fever." I roll over onto my back. "I'm just... thinking. Trying to work something out."

"In your story?"

"Yeah."

"Will it help to talk it out?"

"I don't know. I never have before." I scrub my hand over my face. "I just don't know how to describe something."

"Do you need the internet to research it first? Can you skip over the description until you get back?"

"No. It's a necessary part of my main character's motivation. But I'm having trouble being precise."

"Well," she says, settling cross-legged on the floor next to me, "I'm good for bouncing ideas off of, if you want."

I go up on my elbows and see her gaze dart to where my shirt has ridden up on my stomach. The tip of her tongue touches her upper lip, as if she's picturing licking or kissing that spot, and that immediately makes me feel better about the whole damn world. "It's just...love."

Her widened gaze flies back to my face. "What?"

"In my book. Or *not* in my books. A few weeks ago, I read a review of my last release—"

She sucks in a breath. "Even I know not to do that."

"Normally I wouldn't. But I've followed her blog for a while and our tastes are similar. So when she recommends something, I know I'll probably like it."

"Then your book shows up in her feed and you can't help yourself?"

That's exactly what happened. "It was actually a good review. Four out of five. And she said that she likes my work in general, but that she'd realized what was missing in all my books—because the main characters are all loners, and although some of them have people they care for and some have others they protect, there's never anyone in the story that they actually love. And if they *have* loved, that person's always gone and grief is all that's left. But she said at least the grief offers the characters some emotional depth that might otherwise be missing, since they don't love anyone else within the story."

"Was she right?"

I nod.

"Well, what are your characters fighting for?"

I run a mental tally of my books. "Let's see. Survival. Protecting innocents. Revenge. Saving the world. Some of those get doubled up, depending on the story."

"And your heroes have no family?"

"If they do, they're always estranged." I shrug. "I write loners."

"But if that's what you're good at…do you really intend to change what you're doing based on one review?"

"Not because of the review, but because I think she's right. My books are missing something."

Abbie stares off into the distance, as if she's thinking it over. "But is love really that necessary for a good story?" she finally says. "In *Alien*, no one loved each other. They were just all friends and colleagues. Even in the second movie, there's the little girl who stands in for a daughter, but I'm not sure Ripley actually *loves* her. Cares for her, yes. Feels responsible for her, yes. And maybe there's love between some of the Marines—like the kind of love that's between brothers—but if there is, it's never explored that deeply."

"I agree it's not necessary in every story. Maybe not even necessary in six stories." I glance at the six books on Harris's shelf, telling her exactly which ones I'm talking about. "But when I think of my own favorites…yeah. It's there. Sometimes love for a child, sometimes for a romantic partner. One is love for a dog. So I think that my own can be better—and it'll add that extra danger and emotional punch. I'm not satisfied with just being good enough."

Especially when I *know* my work could be something more. When *I* could be something more. I'd already been considering this, ever since I read that review. But especially after meeting Abbie, it feels even more important. It's not enough to coast along as I have been.

She regards me, her gaze shining with admiration. "So you want to improve. You're asking yourself to do better."

"Yeah, I want to do better. Not for money or sales, though I wouldn't cry over that. But just to look at my work and say that it's better than it was."

With a glance back at her easel, she says, "I know that feeling very well."

"You might also know my current feeling of thinking that I've created an absolute pile of shit."

She laughs. "I'm familiar with that, too."

I lie on the floor again, willing my brain to start working. "I just don't know how to describe what's missing. I don't even think I've ever felt it."

"You've never loved anyone? Or felt loved?"

"No."

"I..." She trails off with a frown. "That's sad."

"So are my books, apparently."

She huffs out a laugh. "What are you doing to fix it? Are you working in a romantic relationship for your main character—or adding a family member? A friend?"

"I gave her a kid. That seems simplest."

"A kid? Is there anyone in the lover category?"

"He's already dead. I still need that grief to have any emotional depth," I say bitterly.

"Did you let that line get to you? Stop it." She nudges my shoulder. "Change it up and make it a divorce. Make her grieve a relationship, but not the person. Maybe she's glad to be rid of him."

"Huh. Divorce is a pretty good idea." I'm already working that through. "Then I can kill the ex in the sewer scene instead of using the neighbor."

"Will it have more impact on the heroine that way?"

"Yeah."

"That sounds like a winner, then. So what else are you struggling with?"

"I suppose it's the components of how she feels about her kid. And at what point all those components become something called love."

"Just say she loves the kid."

"I like to be precise. You love the smell of pine. You also love a cat. The words are the same but they don't mean the same thing."

"Ah. You don't make things easy on yourself."

"Your work would also be easier if you didn't bother to get the lighting and shading right."

"Touché." She stretches out on the floor next to me, then scoots in to use my shoulder as a pillow. "So how old is the kid?"

"Five. Old enough to hide when I need him out of the way, not old enough to survive on his own. Why?"

"Because the components are different. For a baby or a toddler, there's not going to be the aspect of friendship that might develop between, say, a teenager and his mother. What about your mom? When you were five—or later—you didn't feel like she loved you?"

"I don't know. Maybe she did." I pause as Hot Biscuit Slim decides to join us, ambling up onto my chest. "I don't recall her being very affectionate. But I also remember my dad telling her not to coddle me. So maybe she tried, and I just don't remember."

"And you don't love your dad?"

"No."

"Did you ever?"

"I don't think so. Do you love your mom?"

"Of course. I don't like her very much, though."

"That doesn't make any damn sense to me."

"I think…those components are just different." She frowns and absently strokes her hand down Hot Biscuit Slim's back. The cat jumps off my chest and curls up against my other side—out of her reach. "He's such an asshole."

"But you love him."

"I do." Her gaze sharpens again. "Probably a lot like people love babies. Because what is there to love? They poop and spit up and eat and cry. But people love their babies anyway. That component is just…it's adoration, I think. Feeling that this little thing is so perfect, even though it does all these things that would be absolutely irritating if anyone else did it. And even the gross things are also somewhat adorable because the baby—or the cat—is doing them. So I think for a character with a five year old, there'd still be some element of adoration left. Because the kid will have more of a personality to love by then, so genuine affection will start replacing that adoration. Or if not replacing, then growing more equal in weight."

"That makes sense. What if the kid is a spoiled little shit?" The kind who would rip up a little girl's drawing.

"Then she might have to work harder to love him. And there might be more components that are less about love and more about duty and responsibility. Because I think most parents feel an obligation to care for their kids—but there's a difference between taking care of someone because it's the right thing to do, and actually caring about someone, so you take care of them out of love."

"So the action looks the same—feeding, clothing, nurturing—but the motivation is different."

"Yep." She tilts her head back to look at me. "Like when I took care of you. It was just my duty as a human being. Now, though, I'd do it because I care about you." She blinks once, twice, then says in a rush, "Not that I—"

"Love me?"

"No." Her face flushes.

"It's probably too soon."

"For sure."

I look up at the ceiling and grin. Because she cares about me. And I fucking adore her. "What if I wanted to write a character falling in love? What's the difference there?"

She purses her lips as she considers. "I actually think that romantic love is like…okay, here's familial love"—she draws a vertical line in the air—"and next to it is friendship, and then over on the other side of friendship is romantic love. And there's sometimes overlap between familial love and friendship, especially as children get older and they become friends with their parents or siblings. Or it might be like whatever you feel for Harris, if you think of him as a brother."

"Huh. So maybe I do love someone."

"Congratulations. You're now a real human boy."

"Thank you. And romantic love? You put it closer to friendship than family."

"Because there's a ton of overlap between friendship and romantic love. I think being in love *looks* a lot like friendship, but with more components—like adoration, though a more mature version than what you'd feel for a baby. And desire. But not mere lustful desire. Instead it's a desire to be *with* that person. Not always in a sexual way."

"And you've had some experience with this?"

"I thought I was in love a few times. Not that it ever lasted. I think because it was missing a genuine friendship overlap. And maybe with years and marriage, there ends up being more overlap with familial love, too. But probably not at the beginning stages. And I think there's also a component of gratitude when the romantic love is reciprocated? Not in the sense of 'oh, thank goodness someone loves me,' but a sense of being glad that specific person loves you? I don't know, I can't describe it correctly. And there's another component that I *know* is there, kind of related to gratitude, but I can't put my finger on it."

"You've done a hell of a lot better putting your fingers on

these components than I could have. Thank you for that."

"Did it help?"

"It does." A lot more than she knows. "Though I still don't understand the loving but not liking thing with your mom. You're saying you've got familial love with no friend-ship overlap?"

"*Zero* friendship overlap, yes."

"But there's also a hefty dose of obligation and duty tied up with familial love."

She sighs and nods.

"And sometimes love is the source of that duty and obli-gation—like when you care about someone—but sometimes it's just plain old duty because of familial bonds and a shared history or human decency. Not actually love."

Abbie goes quiet. And when she says, "Yeah," her voice wavers.

Then that's enough of this. I kiss her, then haul her up and carry her to the bed, where I get real busy with my mouth and hands.

I FEEL A WHOLE LOT better when I tackle my chapter again after dinner, and the book already seems less shitty. I close the file feeling pleased with how much stronger it all is, dump my headphones and look for Abbie. She's standing by the sink washing her paintbrushes.

She tilts her head toward the easel. "I'm done if you want to look."

Hell yes, I do. I head over and she joins me, standing

back to eye it critically while I get in close. "I knew you were adding a tail," I say after a second. "But I didn't expect that showing just the tip would convey how *big* the monster is. It's obviously huge. You don't show that. Yet somehow I know it is. You're fucking incredible."

"Should I rename it 'Just the Tip'?"

Deflecting again. Because she doesn't know what to do with a genuine compliment. I want to wring Angela Walker's skinny fucking neck.

"You can sell it to me." Her face goes pink and I stand back with her, taking in the whole. "For someone who doesn't like fiction...*this* is fiction. Just in a visual format."

"I never said I don't like fiction. I just don't read it. But I don't only watch documentaries. And I *love* fantasy art. Even fantasy art on *fiction* books," she says with an affected shudder. "Sci-fi covers, the covers of pulp magazines. And I like horror movies, too."

"Now we're talking. What's your very favorite?"

"How does anyone decide something like that?"

"If it's playing, you stop and watch it, every time. Even if you come in during the middle or the end."

"Ah." Her eyes narrow as she thinks. "*Dog Soldiers*. Maybe *The Descent*."

"Fuck yeah. You like horror like I like horror: isolated locations, a group fighting for their lives against monsters, no hope of outside help."

"That's a fairly accurate summary of my overall preference. What's your favorite?"

"*The Thing.*"

She nods. "That's high on my list, too. And it's especially appropriate in an isolated and snowbound cabin. Your megafauna zombies—is that kind of like *The Thing*?"

"There's some heavy inspiration. My book ends a little more happily, though."

"Hey! Spoiler."

"You can't be spoiled for a fiction book you'll never read."

"Maybe I'll make an exception." She stoops down between the armchairs and hauls out Harris's collection.

Oh shit.

One by one, she begins sorting through them, examining the covers. "You write as Xander Bryant? Not James?"

"Not James." Though my heart's thundering, I have to grin at that. "My middle name is Alexander. Bryant is my mother's maiden name. It was going to be Alex Bryant but my agent said Xander was more memorable. And some other Alex Bryant had already taken the website. But I could get Xander Bryant dot com."

She laughs and nods. "The website truly is the most important thing. So Harris…he brings these out here? Or you do?" she asks, just as she flips open the front cover where I've scrawled my signature and a "GO FUCK YOURSELF" to Harris on the title page.

"He does."

"You haven't told any of your other friends what you do?"

"Not really, no."

"You might want to consider dropping the anonymity."

She turns to a back cover. "If you slapped your picture on here, you'd sell more. I'm utterly serious," she adds when I start laughing.

I shake my head. "Thank you. But no."

"Can I read one—" She breaks off when I groan. "If you prefer not, I'll respect that. I know what it's like not to want to expose a part of yourself."

"That's not why. It's just…we might be enemies again."

Her brows arch. "Did we stop?"

"You *like* having an enemy." How did I not realize that before?

She lifts one shoulder in a casual shrug. "It's fun. Especially now that I don't despise you."

"Not at the moment." I hand her my first book.

She gives me a wondering look before sliding her palm over the front cover, where *SHARP LITTLE TEETH* is written in big, chalked letters. Underneath is the tagline: *This family is out for blood.*

"I like the layout and the font. Very nice. And the chalkboard as the background—is it about a schoolteacher?" She flips the book around and begins reading aloud from the cover copy before I can answer. "'There's something odd about the Walter family. The doting mother. The angelic daughters. The persistent whispers about what happened to the father. But in the remote mountain town of Rocky Point, baseless rumors are always flying—and science teacher Neil Sharpe has more pressing concerns. Still mired in the grief of losing the woman he had hoped to spend his life with"'—she tosses me a laughing glance—"'now there's a dangerous new virus sweeping the town. Children are missing classes…or simply missing. Mutilated animals keep appearing on school grounds. The Walter family is the least of Neil's problems…until one tiny bite changes everything.'"

I cringe all the way through. When she finishes, she continues staring at the back cover—then suddenly chortles.

"Hold up! What is this quote? *'The horrors persist but so do I' could be the slogan for Bryant's grieving Neil Sharpe, who must fight his own demons while locked in a desperate battle against an ancient evil. A brilliant and pulse pounding debut from an exciting new author.* What?! I mean, 'brilliant and pulse pounding' is great but— 'The horrors persist'? Is that from the meme with the guinea pig in a pink car? Who is this guy that gave you this quote?"

"He's actually a big name in horror. Since I was a total unknown, my editor sent it to her other authors, so I was lucky to get that. But…yeah. I never asked about the meme, but I wondered, too."

"Oh, that's just the best thing ever." She wipes her eyes. "I'm going to get it on a T-shirt now. Is the description accurate—this is what's in the book?"

I stiffen. "Yes."

"You made us vampires?"

My neck's so rigid, it feels like my head will break off when I nod.

She begins giggling again.

Relief eases the tension that locked me down. "The

real villain is the mother. The girls are just sad and creepy. And the hero's father is a raging narcissist and serves as the secondary villain—because he was the only one around when Neil's fiancée was killed in an accident before the story opens."

"Oooh. Was it really an accident?"

"I guess you'll find out."

"Where's his mother?"

"Long dead. But also accidentally killed."

"I'm *definitely* reading this. Is it your first book?"

"Yeah. I'll admit it's a bit rough around the edges. I also think writing it was just…therapy. Or at least cathartic. None of the others have been so close to home. Though there's always some of me in each book. You're really going to read it? You don't have to for my sake."

"Maybe it'll be therapy for me, too," she says quietly, then looks to the stack still on the side table and suddenly smiles.

"What is it?"

"It's just, when I first saw them here, I thought: horror isn't exactly the best thing to read when you're out in the woods, all alone. Yet here I am. About to read one."

"True. But you're not alone now, are you?"

Abbie

Over the next day, I think of that again and again. *You're not alone now, are you?* Because I came out here to be alone. And yet Reed telling me that I'm not alone feels like the most comforting thing that's ever been said.

Maybe because I wasn't just seeking solitude—I was seeking safety. And I found that here, even though I'm not alone. Because *he* is what feels safe now.

Reed Knowles.

He's working at the table when I finish his book after dinner, then sit staring into the fire. I can see exactly what he means about catharsis—although his catharsis probably looked different. But there's so much in the story that resonates with me. Sometimes painfully. Probably because there's so much truth in what he's written. So much truth, in a book about vampires.

I don't know if I'll give fiction in general another whirl. But I'll definitely keep reading his.

And I can't hear him typing. I peek around the side of my armchair, find him looking at me, his headphones set aside. So he's done for the night. I hold up his book.

"I finished. Can I tell you something?"

"Sure." He rises from the table. "Especially if you tell me that after reading my dulcet prose, you've fallen violently in love with me."

Blindsided. "Do you *want* me to fall in love with you?"

He stops dead in the center of the cabin. Staring at me. First with surprise—because I'm guessing he threw out that violently in love thing as a self-deprecating joke, considering that he'd called the book rough around the edges, but he wasn't expecting my response—then with a sudden, piercing longing.

As if he *does* want me to fall in love with him.

I don't know what to do. Or say. My heart's hammering away—with excitement or terror. I'm not sure which. Maybe both.

Reed blinks. The longing recedes and his gaze sharpens. Perhaps seeing my own startled response. "Too soon?" he says gruffly.

I nod. Trying to catch my breath. "Too soon."

"So we're talking about the book?"

"If you don't mind."

"I don't mind." He scoops me out of my chair, turns and sits—holding me curled up on his lap. I feel like my heart rate might never calm down. "This all right?"

"Yes." More than all right. "Hot Biscuit Slim might get jealous, though."

"Let him. So are you about to throw that book into the fire?"

"No. I liked it. And I see what you mean—about it being therapy. It was a little bit for me, too. Especially…in deciding what to do."

"About your mom?"

I lay my head on his shoulder. Partially because I love the way he's holding me, partially to hide my face. "There was a passage in there about the vampire mother. It went something like, *'Sometimes the world is a better place when someone is born into it. And sometimes the world is a better place after someone leaves it.'* And so I was thinking about my mom and—"

His hand tightens on my knee. "I didn't mean that your mom should die, Abbie."

"Oh, I know. But I think it's accurate in the sense of *my* world. That *my* personal world will be better without certain people in it. And that includes her."

He presses a kiss into my hair. And though he doesn't say anything—

You're not alone now, are you?

"I'm also a little angry with myself for ever getting into this position, because why did I believe her in the first place? She lies. I *know* she lies. And about the stupidest things. Or anything that might make her look bad. Is she running late because she overslept? It's not her fault, it was traffic, she'll say. And everyone lies sometimes, but she does it *all* the time. So why did I believe her about the fucking taxes?"

"Because she had a bill from the county to show you. And she had a good story."

"But she *always* has a story. Do you know she tells people that she's living with me because *I* need the help, financially?"

"What the hell?"

"Yeah," I say flatly. "One of the teachers at MCS is married to the office manager at one of our partner clinics. And she's a friend, so every once in a while, I hear things my mom has said. That one I heard about because my friend asked if I want her to put in a word to Harris about giving me a raise."

"Jesus. What did you tell her?"

"I told her I'm fine. That I'm not in financial trouble. Though I'm sure she thought I was only saying that out of embarrassment." I shrug. "What *could* I say? That my mom constantly lies and tells stories that she believes will make her look good? I'd bet anything that when this vacation is over, I'll find out that she told people that I'm not at home over the holidays because she thought I was working too hard and so she suggested a getaway for me…and then she sent me here on her dime. I'd bet *anything*. Argh!"

I cover my face with my hands, breathing heavily, while Reed holds me tight.

You're not alone now, are you?

I draw in a deep breath before continuing more calmly.

"But you know what's weird? As much as it hurts to know how she lied and took advantage of me, it's also a relief? I felt lighter the other day, after we came back from getting the tree, and I didn't know why. But I figured it out. It's because she stepped over a line. *Way* over. Just like Neil's dad stepped way over a line in your book. Not that my mom killed anyone. But, still."

"Now you don't have to feel so bad when you tell her to get the fuck out of your life."

"Yes! Because there was always so much *guilt*. I was this terrible, terrible person for even *thinking* of wanting them to leave. But now…she told this horrible, inexcusable lie. And I'm glad!" I laugh. "I'm so glad! Because now I can tell her she has two months to find a new place, and there's nothing she can say in her defense! There's no way to gaslight me on this. So I'm just…fuck, yes! Am I a terrible person?"

"No," Reed says. "I think you're just about perfect."

"Even when I'm singing?"

"Especially when you're singing. In fact, I think we need the next verse of that song right now." He stands up out of the chair with me wrapped around him. "Are we on the fifth fuck of Christmas? Five golden rings is usually the part where it becomes a power ballad."

"So… ♪On the fifth fuck of Christmas, my enemy gave to me…*HOPEFULLY NOT A DISEASE!*♪" I belt the line out at the top of my lungs, and Reed has to stop, face buried in my shoulder as he laughs.

Finally he shakes his head. "You've got to have a number

in the lyric."

"Okay, okay— ♪*FIVE PUSSY LICKINGS!*♪"

"That, I can do," he says, and lowers me to the bed. "I adore your pussy. I adore *you*, too."

I catch my breath, staring up at him. How does he keep doing this to me? But he doesn't let me respond. Instead he begins kissing me, and all I can think is that he adores me. *He adores me.* And no one has ever adored me before.

"Reed," I whisper when he begins sliding down. "Can I tell your head where to go?"

"You can," he says, nipping my belly, his fingers skimming up the inside of my thigh. "What would you like?"

"For you to use me."

His body tenses against mine, but I can't look at him. "Use you how, Abbie girl?"

"Like there's nothing in the world that you want more than you want me. That you *need* to be inside me. So you'll just bend me over and take everything you want."

"From behind?"

"Yes."

"Rough?"

"However you like."

"I like it all with you." His voice deepens. "But spread your thighs first, so I can get those five pussy lickings in."

He does, five long swipes of his tongue that leave me panting and rocking against his mouth, my hands buried in my hair so that I don't yank on his. Then he's up over me, dragging me to the side of the bed, flipping me onto my stomach.

"Feet on the floor, Abbie girl," he growls against the back of my neck, then uses his own foot to kick them wider. "That's it. Now you just wait."

I can't do anything else. He's fully clothed, his chest against my back, pinning me down into the bed. His big hand slides down over the curve of my ass, fingers stroking through the drenched furrow of my pussy from behind. I whimper, biting my lip.

"You know the one downside to kissing you? To eating your pussy? I can't use my tongue to tell you how goddamn sexy you are." His hot mouth tugs at my earlobe, sending a spike of lust all the way down to my curling toes. "And you asked me for the easiest thing in the world. Because I *do* want you more than anything. I *do* need to be inside you more than anything."

His fingers press deep into my cunt, then he pulls out to slick them down over my clit. My legs are already shaking, and if I wasn't supported by the bed, I'd be flat on the floor.

Probably shaking there, too.

"You don't know what you've done to me, do you?" His fingers sink into me again and I bite the quilt beneath me, holding in my scream. "How I think about getting into you every fucking minute. I don't even know myself anymore, this person inside me who can't think of anything but holding you, kissing you, fucking you. You've done something to me. Made me someone else. Someone who *needs* this pussy. Now, are you going to be a good girl and let me have it?"

"Yes," I say but it's barely a moan into the blanket.

"What was that?" His fingers rub over my clit again before he gives my pussy a gentle slap. I gasp for air, my head shooting back, my ass jerking up. His free hand circles my throat—lightly, not cutting off my breathing, and his thumb in that spot below my ear that drives me out of my mind. "Will you hold still and let me use this pussy?"

"Yes! Please, Reed."

The rasp of his zipper is barely louder than my own ragged breaths. The tear of foil comes next. My inner muscles clench.

"But what if I don't put it on?" he rumbles against my ear. I know he has. I can feel the slickness of the condom's lubrication as he drags the head of his cock down the split of my ass, aiming for my cunt. "Maybe I'll just use this pussy how I want to—skin to skin, then filling you with my cum. Should I do that, Abbie girl?"

I always love where his head goes. "Please don't," I tell him, even as I'm nodding.

"Too late." The delicious stretching pressure builds at my entrance before my flesh yields and he thrusts deep. I cry out, the pleasure overwhelming me as his thick groan fills the air. "You feel me inside you now? My bare cock deep inside you? But fuck, it's not enough. Need to get deeper. Up on your toes. Let me all the way in."

He rears back, gripping my hips and hiking me up. His cock slams deep, so deep. Again and again. I can't do anything but take it, can't move, can't think as my body seems to twist tighter and tighter from the outside in.

"Play with your clit now, Abbie girl. You think me getting into this pussy is enough? Fuck, no. I want to feel you squeeze me tight, so goddamn tight. I want to feel you get so fucking wet, the way you do when you come. Go on, now. That's right. Fuck. Rub that hot little clit nice and fast. Oh, fuck. You're tightening around my cock. Tightening. You about to come? Fuck yes. Ohhhhh *fuck*."

He groans out the last as I begin to come, writhing against the mattress, my hand trapped under my pussy. The speed of his thrusts increases, sending stars shooting behind my eyes as my inner walls convulse around his pistoning shaft.

"So good. So fucking good." His hands flatten on either side of my shoulders, his thick cock still pumping gently into me. "But I'm going to use this pussy nice and slow now, yeah? I want your thigh up like this—yeahhh. You're so perfect, Abbie. So fucking perfect."

He brings my right knee up onto the bed, spreading me for his deep and slow thrusts. Tension and arousal begin twisting together inside me again.

"Can you rub your clit some more?"

"Can't. My hand's cramping like this." The lingering pleasure slurs my words a little.

Reed chuckles and kisses the back of my neck. Then his fingers replace mine, slippery and sliding over my clit while his cock fucks into me slow, so slow, building the next orgasm into a soul-shattering roll of thunder. This time he follows me over, his flesh spasming inside me, making me hold him tight within. So tight.

We lay there with him softening inside me, his chest heaving against my back. "That was all right, Abbie girl?"

"Perfect," I mumble sleepily.

"For me, too."

Then he has to pull away to get rid of the rubber, and I go clean up. Perhaps that should have broken the mood. But a few minutes later I'm back in his arms. Still warm and safe and sleepy.

You're not alone now, are you?

I'm not.

But I try not think of what I'll be when this holiday is over.

Reed

"I THINK THEY'RE BOTH DONE."

I glance over to where Abbie has a canvas propped on each armchair. It's New Year's Eve—the last night I'm supposed to be here, since the snow has mostly melted. In the past few days, when we haven't been hiking or lazing or reading, she's been busy painting, putting in as many hours as I have been writing.

But not adding to a thrift store canvas. Instead she took two of the canvases she'd brought and completely painted over them. So both of these paintings are all hers.

She's quiet as I look. I don't need her to tell me what they are. One for her sister. One for her mom. Though they aren't the subjects. They aren't portraits. Instead one is red and raw, blood dripping from skin that's been constantly picked at. The other depicts a small, elegantly decorated room that almost echoes with a sense of emptiness.

"Do you intend to give these to them?"

"Probably not." She smiles a little. Maybe imagining their reactions. "It was just…therapy."

I kiss her for that. She laughs against my mouth before turning to regard the paintings again, her eyes gleaming with a mischievous light. "Should we leave them for Harris? Next to your books?"

"As thanks for letting you stay?"

She wrinkles her nose. "He might not appreciate the bloody one."

"I would. If you don't want them, I'll buy them." And have another part of her with me. It's a constant ache, not knowing whether a few paintings will be all that I have of her after today. "I've already started a collection."

She leans into me, resting her head against my shoulder. "I think I'll hold onto them for a little while. I do love the thrift store ones. But it felt good to use the entire canvas again. To make something fully mine. I'd forgotten *how* good." With a heavy sigh she adds, "And having these around might help me remember why I need to stand firm. When I'm in the middle of it."

Of all the shit she's about to go through. "I hate that you'll have to go through that."

"I do, too. But…I have to."

She's staring at her mother's painting. And though she doesn't say a word, I can tell that she's hurting.

"Abbie?"

"I know you said you don't love your father. What *do*

you feel for him?"

"Frustration. Revulsion."

"There's no respect left at all?"

"No. Do you think I should?"

She shakes her head, then exhales a shaky breath. "I just…I don't know if I truly love my mother anymore. And I feel like such a bad person for even saying it. I care, because how can I not? But there's no respect left. And no trust. It seems that all that's left in me is a sense of duty and obligation—and even *that*, she's broken. With her lies and just…everything. She's not someone I want to be around. And there's still the relief that I have reason to make her go, but this. This. Not *loving* her anymore. It feels…it just feels as if I'm *so* horrible."

"Do you think I'm horrible for not loving my father?"

With the back of her hand, she wipes her eyes. "No."

"Then give yourself the same clemency as you do me, Abbie girl. What about your sister?"

She pulls in a deep breath, visibly calming herself. "I still love her. Maybe there's just more there between us to begin with."

"Will you be giving her the option to stay with you?"

"No," she says, and I have to conceal my relief. Because it's not my decision, but it was the one I hoped Abbie would make for her own sake. "Because everything she does is still so hurtful. I don't want to live with that. And it's not like I'm kicking her out onto the street. She'll still have a place with my mom." She blows out a breath that puffs her cheeks. "But I think I'll always hope for more, because I'd like my sister to be a friend again. You know she wasn't always so negative?"

"No?"

"And I've thought on it a lot more since I vented to you last week. Thinking about *why* she became this way."

"What did you come up with?"

"I think she retreated into hating everything because it's safe. Isn't it? It's like armor. Because if you like something or someone—or love them—you can be hurt. Disappointed. And that goes for so many things. Those favorite books you have as a kid, then you find out the author's a bigot or a sleazeball. And if you like someone's music? Well fuck, he's a rapist. And that politician you supported and voted for backs down on every issue he campaigned on now that he's in office, never puts up a fight, never calls out the political bullshit that should be called out. So if Lauryn hates everything, well…instead of being disappointed, she's proven right when something turns out shitty. And it protects her from being judged the way she judges other people."

"Sounds like a real unhappy way to live."

"It does. And if it's true, I feel bad for her. And sad for her. But protecting herself doesn't excuse how she hurts me while doing it."

"No, it doesn't." Nothing could fucking excuse it. But she's not my sister…and I could imagine taking a whole lot of shit from Harris before making that break.

"Though I understand the need to retreat. That desire for

safety. Obviously, since I'm here. No one has the energy to always fight. Everyone has to recharge. But then you have to try again—not just stay where it's easy to stay."

"So you're saying cynicism and negativity is for cowards and weaklings," I say to make her laugh.

And she does, bumping against my side. "Not *everything* negative. There's nothing wrong with expressing an opinion or not liking something—though of course there's always a time and place. And things that hurt other people *should* be called out. Not all cynicism is bad, either. Only when there's no attempt at anything else. But it has its place, too. Like, I'd be a complete fool to think that, after I tell my mom that I caught her out in her lies—*Well, she learned her lesson and she'll never do that again!* But hope in general isn't foolish. I think hope takes far more courage than cynicism does."

"What of love? Love takes more courage, too, yeah?"

She narrows her eyes at me. "Are you thinking of your book?"

"A little." I always am, a little—which Abbie picked up on days ago. I know she's not offended now by the tangent because she likes it when I bounce ideas off her. "Because I like that as a theme: Blanket cynicism and negativity is a coward's refuge. That might be what my heroine is truly fighting against. A monster is never enough. There has to be something else, the thing that's the *real* horror—or what that horror represents. But I'll have to work out how. Either she'll be fighting her own cynicism or it'll be someone else who is the cynic, someone who has more power than she does. But she has enough strength to hope and love, so she uses that strength to win. Or maybe hope and love *give* her strength. Something."

"It sounds like it'll be a good fight."

Fuck, my chest keeps knotting up. Because I'm hoping, too.

"I think it will be," I tell her.

I don't want this to end. Yet the end's crawling closer. I hold Abbie in my lap with her head against my shoulder—we've both got real comfortable with this position over the past week—and battle everything within me. Everything that wants to hold her tighter and tighter.

Because that first night, I'd promised to go as soon as I could. We figured that would be around New Year's. Today, we both agreed the roads are probably passable now. And the whole fucking reason Abbie came out here was to be by herself. Being stuck together here didn't turn out as disastrous as we both thought it would…yet she hasn't said anything about me staying longer. Hasn't said anything about what happens after we leave this cabin.

At least, she hasn't said anything about what happens between *us*. She's told me what's coming for her, otherwise. She has to go back. She has to clean house. She has to withstand all the shit her family is going to throw at her over the next two months. Maybe longer. And although I want—fucking *need*—to stand with her, to help her through, it's got to be her choice. Because *me* being there with her might make everything a million times worse. I know exactly the shit they'd give her for being with someone named Knowles. Abbie has to know, too.

What I don't know is whether she'll decide I'm worth it.

So I wait. And I hope.

"Did you plan anything specific for tonight?" I ask her, and my throat feels raw and thick.

"No." Her breath against my neck is the sweetest damn thing. "No fireworks, for obvious reasons. I don't like champagne. I think there's some old tradition of opening the door to let the old year out and usher the new year in, so I suppose we could do that."

"Usher it into Harris's cabin?"

I feel her smile against my throat. "Symbolically."

"What did you do last year?"

"I volunteered to be Harris's plus one at the Bennet gala, because I was avoiding home."

Not what she normally does, then. "The year before that?"

"I was in bed, binge-watching...I think it was *The Last of Us*."

"That sounds close to what I did. I might have already been asleep when it hit midnight."

"Well, I've never been kissed at midnight on New Year's Eve, so that's what you're doing tonight."

"Yes, ma'am."

She laughs, then lifts her head. "What is Hot Biscuit Slim looking at?"

At the window. It's too late for it to be the birds that he's usually chirping at.

Abbie uncurls from my lap and I follow her over, looking out.

"Oh," she breathes softly. "Are those deer or elk?"

"Elk." A small herd in the clearing, bathed in moonlight.

Watching them, she reaches down and entwines her fingers with mine. "It might hurt your professional ego to hear, but nature is the very best structural engineer."

"I happen to agree. What about Paul Bunyan, though—making those rivers?"

"He's a close second to nature."

"Then I won't argue against that, either. But what made you think of it?"

"Looking at the elk. Which made me start thinking of meese legs—"

"Meese legs?"

"Yeah. A moose has four legs, so it's a plural number of legs, so meese legs."

Her straight face never breaks. It's fucking incredible how she does that. "All right," I tell her. "Go on."

"Well, the fat cells in a moose's legs are mostly unsaturated, so they don't harden as quickly at low temperatures as saturated fats do. The cells don't line up in their orderly crystals or bricks or whatever, so they don't freeze unless it's really, really cold. I don't know if elk legs are the same. Maybe? Probably something similar. And I just think it's amazing."

She is amazing. The way she looks at the world, searching for all the wonder in it. And my heart's aching so fucking bad. Because I think I know what love is now. And understand why it's so hard to name all of the components. It's made up of too many words, none of them exactly precise, but all of them right.

I cup her face in my hands, capture her mouth in a brief, soft kiss.

"Is it midnight?" she whispers.

"I'll still be kissing you then. Though not only on your mouth." I sweep her up, carry her across the cabin. "This will be the last condom. Though I don't know how you'll top the eleven fuckers sucking."

"With a dozen cunts a-coming, of course."

Of course. I kiss her, then kiss her again. The last one. It won't be enough. It can't be enough. One last night won't get me through a week, let alone the rest of my life. But it *won't* be the last.

I'll have hope.

It's LONG AFTER MIDNIGHT, BUT Abbie wraps a blanket around herself and goes to open the door—then stands there, breathing deep. Though it's not as cold as it was, the nighttime air still freezes our breath. I wrap my arms around her, loving the way she leans back against my chest.

"All right?"

"Yes." Despite that answer, she seems quiet. Pensive. After a short while, she finally says, "Do you need to get back home right away? Do you have anything scheduled before Monday?"

My heart pounds. "I don't have anything until the middle of the month. Are you asking for a reason?"

"The snow is mostly gone here." She gestures to the clearing in front of the cabin. "But there's still quite a bit under the trees where the sun didn't reach. And I didn't really enjoy driving through the snow coming out this way. Even with the chains. I know you said your truck isn't far away but—"

"Yes. I'll stay."

"So the snow can melt some more."

"Right." I brush her hair away from her nape, breathe in her skin, then kiss the sensitive little spot under her ear. "Mouth and hands until then?"

"Yes," she says with a little moan.

And closes the door.

Abbie

I HAVE TO GO BACK.

That knowledge is just as horrible now as it was before, though for an entirely different reason. I'm not looking forward to confronting my mother, but I've steeled myself. Readied myself.

I'm not ready to let go of Reed.

He's been quiet all morning. First in bed, where—instead of being as vocal as he usually is while I'm sucking his cock— he only watched me, his eyes locked with mine, stroking his thumb down my cheek before murmuring that I'm so damn beautiful. He was almost wordless while helping me pack the car, though he spoke up and offered to drive when I looked doubtfully at the road, which is still muddy and slushy, with snow piled in deep patches under the trees.

Now he silently drives while I watch him. Memorizing his profile. Wishing that I'd sketched him. Hoping my memory will be good enough.

Praying I won't need to rely on my memory.

But he hasn't said anything about the future. Not even a hint. And how can I ask him? How can I say, "Hey, do you want to be with me while I deliberately set fire to a huge portion of my life, especially during these next few months when I'll probably need to cling to you and cry a lot and work through tons of emotional baggage?" Even if I did ask, would he only feel obligated because I took care of him and let him eat my food and also fucked him a dozen times? I don't even know how to bring up the topic of us still seeing each other without acknowledging that *he* would be dealing with shit, too. I can so easily imagine the insulting crap that my mother and sister might say to him. To his face.

How can I ask him to walk into a situation like that?— especially after he's already had to deal with so much of my mom's bullshit over the years? I don't know if I *can* ask. Or if it's *wrong* to ask someone to bear that. And I don't have time to figure it out. This drive won't even last the hours until we reach the city, because his truck is at his dad's lodge somewhere nearby.

Then there it is. A sprawling log house—empty and shuttered. The new family gathering apparently didn't last through New Year's Day. I wonder if Reed's dad ever found out about the "Oops." Then realize I don't really care.

Because we're stopping next to his truck. Reed's jaw is set as he puts the car into park. Hot Biscuit Slim yowls angrily from his carrier.

"We're here," he says, and gets out of the car.

Blindsiding me. I thought there'd be at least a kiss. Something. But I can't joke this time. Numbly I get out of the passenger side while he grabs his pack from the back.

I'm still standing there, between my car and his truck, as Reed comes around to his vehicle's door. He looks down at me, and I've gotten good at reading his face. But I can't read it now.

"Thanks for driving." I can barely get it out.

His nod is abrupt. As if he just wants to get the hell out of here. "Thanks for taking care of me."

I'm *not* going to cry. "Of course. Oh! Wait. I have that painting to give you. The kaiju—" I stop, because he looks absolutely stricken. My heart drops to the ground somewhere near my feet, smashing and freezing. "Do you not want it?"

"No. Yes. But I meant to—" A muscle in his jaw works and he looks away. "I was going to call you about it later. About buying it."

"But I want to give it."

"Yeah, but..." His eyes close. "I wanted a reason to call you later."

"Oh," I say in a tiny voice. Not much more than a breath of sound, as all the broken pieces of my heart begin reassembling.

Reed turns and tosses his pack into his truck before facing me again, shoving his fists into his pockets. "Are you going straight home? Have your confrontation right away?"

"Yes. It's best to just get the first fight over with."

He nods. "Well, if you get there and you're not ready yet, you're always welcome to escape to my place."

"No," I say, and something happens to his face. Something I've seen before—that first night. When he saw the blood on his fingers. The almost stunned realization of an injury.

Because he thinks I won't come to him.

But I don't have time to answer. He makes a deep, wounded noise. Then my face is in his hands and he's kissing me, kissing me desperately, the way I wanted him to in the car. As if he needs me so badly, as if he wants me more than anything, as if he can't bear to let go. And it *is* that, but it's the worst sort of kiss. A ripping, devastating goodbye.

So when he tears his mouth away, I hold tight. Gripping his jacket. Not letting him go.

"Reed. That's not what I— Reed." I urge him down, until his forehead rests against mine, our harsh breaths mingling. "I meant, *no*, I won't put it off. I *will* do it today. I'll stand up for myself. Establish boundaries. That'll be today."

"There's no doubt you can." His throat works. "You're strong as hell, Abbie girl."

I exhale a shuddering breath. "But is the invitation open if I need an escape over these next few months? This cabin is a little far away."

He pulls back. His gaze searches mine and the frantic hope in his eyes makes me want to cry very, very happy tears. "That invitation is always open." He hesitates. "So we're friends, then?"

"Well…" I ponder. "How about frenemies?"

"That's the worst fucking word," he says, but he's grinning.

"The best words are the ones you understand perfectly, and frenemies is very clear in its meaning. Plus, it's fun. Oh! Funemies?"

He huffs out a laugh. "Is that what we are?"

"We could spend more time finding out."

He goes still, watching me. "More time? All right, then. I'll be happy with *any* time, if it means I see you again."

"Maybe Valentine's? I'd like to have the best Valentine's ever. I'd need you for that."

"Yeah?" His voice seems suddenly rougher. Thicker. "I can do that."

"So it's a date. But that's about six weeks away. What about—"

"President's Day?"

"Or Twelfth Night."

His brow furrows. "When the hell is Twelfth Night?"

"January fifth, I think. So, tomorrow."

"I've never celebrated it."

"We *have* celebrated it. With condoms. The Twelve Days of Christmas song is actually about that."

"We should celebrate Twelfth Night properly, then. With your whole song."

"We can do that." My heart is practically dancing within my chest. "What are you doing the rest of today?—after I go blow up my life, of course. Aside from that, this could be the best January fourth ever."

"With you, Abbie, I have a feeling that every day will be the best ever."

My eyes suddenly burn with tears. "I have the same feeling about you."

"Good." His hand cups my cheek. "Do you want me to follow you home? Help you unload…and be there when you set those boundaries?"

"No," I tell him, "though I wish I could say yes. But I know the argument would devolve into being about you—and then all the old shit about my dad—instead of focusing on her lies. And honestly, it's not even the confrontation today that I'm dreading. It's what will come after."

What I *know* will come after. When my mom will try every angle to wear me down. First telling me that I'm wrong. Claiming that Reed must have lied to me. That she never actually said his dad stole the house at auction for nothing. And *then* she'll lay on the guilt. Beyond that…I don't know. We never got past the guilt stage, because that was when I would cave.

"Then come to my house afterward. Bring Hot Biscuit Slim."

"My little hideout at your place." I laugh a little. "Maybe I won't even unload my car. We've still got a ton of leftover food."

"Bring it or don't. Either way is fine. And I won't go in with you, but I'll follow you home, yeah? Because the roads might be icy."

I can only silently nod, suddenly overwhelmed with

emotion. Reed bends to kiss me, and it's the sweetest kiss yet. Then he turns toward his truck.

A second later, he turns back again. "It might be too soon, but I *do* want you to. I want you to fall violently in love with me."

"All right." My heart is thundering. "But I want that, too. You, in love with me. Wildly in love with me. I want that more than anything."

"You'll get it, Abbie girl." He stares at me with an almost silly, lopsided grin. "All right, then. We'll figure out all the components of love, yeah? And we'll piss off our families while we do it."

I would laugh, but I can't mistake the concern that comes over him when he says the last part. "Are you worried about your dad?"

"I'm done with my dad. I'm more worried about you. You're living with them now, even if it won't be for long. I don't want them saying hurtful shit to you on my account."

"I'll be all right." Anything they say against Reed will only make me more determined. Nothing they could do or say would make me end this.

Only Reed could.

"Okay, then." His warm hands cradle my face again. "I'll be behind you all the way home. I won't go inside or get in your way. But I'll wait outside until you're done with that first fight. If you want me to look after Hot Biscuit Slim while you're in there, I'll look after him. If you're not up to driving afterward, I'll drive you. If you need anything, I'll be there to help you. You're not alone. Even if you need to do this by yourself, you're not alone. All right?"

I nod. He kisses me again, then I watch him return to his truck through a blur of tears. He stops there, waiting as I get into my car. Making sure that I'm all right. Letting me know I'm not alone.

I start up the engine and wipe away my stupid, grateful tears. Thanking the universe for a blizzard. Two weeks ago, I'd hoped to have the best Christmas ever, but I never could have imagined things would turn out so happily, or that I'd feel so safe and free. And it's all thanks to Reed Knowles. Because I didn't open a single gift this year.

But I still got everything I need.

Reed

Epilogue

Christmas Eve — One Year Later

BALANCING A PLATE OF COOKIES IN MY HAND, I OPEN THE gate between Delia's backyard and Abbie's before noticing the silver car parked at the curb. Fuck. I'd hoped to be with Abbie if Angela and Lauryn showed up uninvited.

I wasn't sure they would. But I should have realized that Angela wouldn't miss an opportunity to play the wounded penitent and to lay on more guilt.

All the shit last year went down pretty much as Abbie had predicted. The gaslighting. Then blaming me. Then apologizing for her lies, while at the same time tossing in excuse after excuse for lying. Then saying it was all a mistake, that Angela never meant to lie—but once she did, she didn't know how to get out of it. Which all added up to Angela not really being sorry for lying, just sorry she got called out.

That was the first week. Then everything at Abbie's house quieted down and it seemed like her mother had accepted Abbie's demand that she find a new place. But, no. That was just Angela pretending or hoping it would all go away. That everything was fine. Two weeks before the deadline, Abbie asked about the house search, and Angela was *shocked* that Abbie truly meant to kick them out.

Then the shit started all over again, but with more added guilt. Angela began claiming that she needs to invest the four hundred K for her retirement, and that it makes more financial sense for all of them to split expenses. Which might be true, except it ignored that Abbie can't fucking bear to live with them.

But then, Abbie's happiness was never something Angela really gave two shits about.

In the end, Angela gave in—but mostly because of Lauryn, who hadn't spoken a word to Abbie since she realized her sister and I were together. But Angela twisted the knife as she went, claiming that Abbie's relationship with me was the true reason they were going. Making it Abbie's fault, laying it all on her shoulders, instead of ever admitting it was her lies that started it.

I can't count how many times Abbie cried in my arms during those two months. And I would hold her, terrified—for her sake and for mine—that the hurt would be too much and she'd give in.

She didn't. Despite everything they put her through. Her strength and her resilience kicked in. That she still burns so brightly after all that is simply fucking incredible to me.

Incredible and humbling, that it was *my* arms she sought when she needed holding.

Then began Angela's desperate but half-assed attempts at redemption. Abbie had told her she had no interest in maintaining a relationship, especially since she can't trust anything Angela says. What followed were long "I'm so sorry" texts that repeated all of the excuses and begged for forgiveness and promised never to lie again. Then every day, she sent a good morning message that said how much she loves and misses Abbie—often accompanied by pictures of Abbie as a kid.

Because she'd known that Abbie's good manners would force her to reply...until Abbie simply didn't anymore. She put her mother's notifications on silent and asked me to read them, instead, and tell her if her mother ever said anything important. About *why* she loved and missed her. Or if she ever apologized without all the excuses.

She never did.

Then came the day when Abbie heard from her friend at work that Angela had taken sick days off for two full weeks, because she was taking care of Lauryn, who was in the hospital with COVID. But when Abbie frantically called Lauryn, her sister was holed up in her bedroom, quarantining herself away from their mother, who was home with a mild case.

That day seemed to melt a little of the ice between Abbie and Lauryn, though not completely. Lauryn texted on Abbie's birthday, which meant a hell of a lot more to Abbie than the slew of texts and photos her mother sent. And Abbie invited Lauryn out to dinner on her sister's birthday, though it fell through when Angela invited herself along, too.

Because after that last lie, Abbie was truly done with her mother's shit. And angry at first, though now more likely to roll her eyes and shake her head.

Not that Angela has accepted it. Abbie is convinced that the pleas for forgiveness and reconciliation are really because her mother's worried that word of their estrangement will get around MCS and put cracks in Angela's goody-goody facade. I suppose it might...if anyone actually cared that much about Angela's relationship with her daughters. As if it would merit more than a shrug and a 'that's a shame.' Angela must believe everyone around her is wholly invested in her life, because I can't imagine what the hell else would drive someone to bother telling so many lies.

And I make a good part of my living writing fiction.

Hot Biscuit Slim is huddled on top of the dryer when I let myself in through the garage. "Hey there, buddy." I scoop him up, holding the cookies far away from his greedy little face. "Did the mean lady scare you away?"

No raised voices, at least. I'm not too worried—Abbie can hold her own—but that doesn't mean she ought to be alone.

I enter through the kitchen and get a deep hit of the

pine scent permeating the house. My own place has that not-lived-in smell now. I'm rarely there. Maybe once a week. I might put it on the market soon. My house is newer but hers has more charm. So we could put the money away for if...*when*...we ever outgrow this one. But it's perfect for us now.

I set the cookies Delia gave to us on the counter and lower Hot Biscuit Slim to the floor. From the living room, I hear Lauryn's voice.

"Where did you get the tree from?"

"From the Morgan tree farm," Abbie says.

"You should have gotten one with live roots. Then it can be replanted."

"We discussed that," I say, stopping in the door between the kitchen and living room. Abbie will let me know if she wants me to stay or go. I keep my eyes on her, partially so I won't miss any cues. Partially because the sight of Angela's pinched mouth makes me want to snatch her up by the scruff and chuck her out the door. "But the Morgan farm is run by someone I know, and it's been a rough year for them. So we decided to buy ours there."

"It can't be too rough," Lauryn scoffs. "All those farms get tax breaks and handouts."

I meet Abbie's gaze. She gives a little roll of her eyes. Telling me it's not worth arguing. And it's not worth justifying our decisions to her sister.

With the patience of a saint, Abbie says instead, "We bought some gift baskets from their farm store. Jams, cookies, cheese. They're in cute little packages if you want something."

"I'm sure you bought them intending them for your *new* friends," Lauryn says, glaring at me.

Ah, so that's what this is about. Two days ago, Abbie got a message from Angela—then Lauryn—that dinner would be at 2 P.M. on Christmas. As if it was a foregone conclusion that Abbie would be spending it with them, though they hadn't celebrated the holiday in years. She replied with a thank you, but she already had other plans.

Which we do. Harris is coming over, along with Delia, if she's feeling up to it after her family visits. A few others might stop by—Abbie's made an effort in the past year to become closer with a couple of her work friends.

Not invited were her family. Or mine.

Though if I ever had to choose, I'd take Lauryn hating me over Karilee getting into the shower with me. And I'm guessing that Angela's pinched lips are because Abbie already declined to go to their house again.

"Christmas is a time for family," Angela abruptly puts in. "And it'll be the first in the new house. You should visit."

"Like you always visit *your* mother for Christmas?"

Lauryn smirks and stops glaring at me to watch her mother and Abbie.

Angela stiffens. "My mother lives hours away. And she understands that my schedule is always too full to visit this time of year."

"Not just this time of year. You've been too busy for all of your family as long as I've been alive."

"That's not fair," Angela protests. "It was *you* who left us here last year to go on your vacation. And this year, you're the one not coming. The one too busy for us."

"I never said I was too busy to come. That's always your excuse. Though I do work two jobs now and I *am* busy—"

"Two jobs?" Her mother cuts in. "I told you that O'Neil man wasn't paying you what you were worth."

"Yes, Harris does. Plus, I have amazing benefits. Don't go down this road again, Mother."

"What's the other job?" Lauryn asks.

"I'm doing freelance work for a local author."

Not even a flicker of an eyelash in my direction. Her poker face will never *not* impress me. And it's true. She's taken over my social media, posting far more frequently than I ever did. But sales really started moving when she painted movie-style posters to promote each of my books. That went over so well that my publisher asked her to create my next cover. Which amused her. Pleased her, too.

Angela frowns. "What local author?"

"I'm not authorized to say. The point is, Mother, that I'm also busy. But I *could* fit in a visit to your new house if I wanted to. After everything that happened last year, I said that I don't want to. That after the way you lied, I no longer feel obligated to. So I'm not sure what you want from me."

"I don't want anything," she sniffs. "Except a little courtesy."

"What courtesy is required beyond saying that I won't make it to your dinner? I'm not telling you to expect me and then not showing up. I'm saying I won't be there. You have your plans, and I very kindly told you that I had my own."

"But you could have included us," Lauryn says.

"Except that you've told me—you've *both* told me!—over and over again, for years and years, that you don't like this kind of Christmas. You don't like the music. You don't like the tree. You don't like the buying and giving of gifts. You certainly don't like my boyfriend and have zero interest in getting to know him. Being here wouldn't make you happy and it wouldn't make me happy. You'll be happier doing Christmas your way; I'll be happier doing it mine."

I'm pretty sure neither of them hears anything beyond Abbie's reference to me.

Lauryn's chin goes up. "Did you invite *his* father, too? That's why you won't include us."

"John Knowles is never getting an invitation here. Lauryn, if you truly want to spend time with me, why not on another day? One where we don't have such different opinions on what we should be doing that day? I'd meet you halfway."

That wasn't directed toward her mother, but I'm not surprised when Angela inserts herself again.

"Where's the halfway now?" Angela demands. "Ever since you've met *him*, you've been like this. Completely immoveable. Utterly unforgiving. Not caring about anyone else's opinions or feelings, as long as you get what you want."

Abbie's eyes go bright with amusement. Oh, but she's pissed, too. A slight lift of her hand keeps me where I am as she replies, "And yet…aren't you here arguing with me because *you* haven't gotten what *you* want?"

"I'm not here to argue."

"No, you're here to bully me and guilt me into submission. Why do you want me to come anyway? Why do you want *me* there? What about me do you actually like? Anything?"

"You're my daughter—"

"A reason that doesn't include the words 'daughter' or 'family.' What is it about *me* that I add to your Christmas? Or any day?"

Either Angela can't think of one or she doesn't understand the question.

Lauryn does, rolling her eyes. "Don't blame her if she can't answer that, Abbie. I doubt anyone in marketing *ever* added anything good to the world."

"What the fuck is wrong with you, Lauryn?" Abbie snaps back, wiping the smirk from her sister's face. "You've got so much fire in you, but why do you always use it to burn people? I honest to god don't know, but I'm really fucking tired of it."

"Abigail Rose! What has gotten into you?"

"*He* has," Lauren says.

"*You* have! You *both* have! Except I've finally stopped taking what you give. And you know what? I have Christmas gifts for you both. Let me go get them."

Lauryn and Angela look at each other when Abbie stomps away into the room she uses as her studio. They don't even glance over to where I'm standing with my shoulder still propped against the kitchen doorframe, just watching them. Waiting for Abbie to signal.

She comes back hauling two canvases. Fuck, yeah. That's my girl.

"Merry Christmas," she says as gives the first to her sister.

Lauryn holds hers out with a grimace. "Is that...blood in a wine glass?"

"It's called 'A Glass of Whine'—the 'h' is silent. All those little pinpricks in the skin are the constant nagging that draws the blood, filling the glass of whine. It's to represent people who only talk to criticize, who never have anything positive to say about anyone or any situation, but still do nothing to help. Who don't even boost the people who are helping. Who just pick and pick and pick, and shit on people who are out there doing their best, because what they do isn't good enough for you—though you don't do fucking anything!"

Her sister recoils a little. "You're saying this is me?"

"I'm saying this is how I feel whenever you talk to me. And here's yours, Mother. It's called 'Take a Long Hard Look.' Merry Christmas."

Angela's brow furrows. "Is that the mirror in the foyer at the old house?"

"It is."

"There's nothing in the reflection."

"Because it represents people who are obsessed with how they appear. Who lie so that they always look good and who try to justify and excuse every shitty thing they do. People whose moral center is empty but at the same time, they're absolutely full of themselves. And they just...

suck people dry. Like vampires."

Angela looks to her in open-mouthed disbelief. "And you're saying that's *me*?"

"Come now, Mother. Do you see yourself reflected in the mirror there?"

I fucking love this woman. While her mother is working that one through and deciding how to respond, I bring Abbie two big cellophane bows. "Don't forget these."

"Oh, good call. Thank you." She slaps a cheery bow on each painting before pointedly opening the front door. "I hope you like your gifts, and I'm so glad you could come over. I won't expect it again, since I know you're very, very, *very* busy, Mother. And Lauryn, I'm sure you've got a long post to write on the Am I The Asshole forum, so I'll let you get to it. Spoiler alert: YTA."

Sometimes I forget how acid her tongue can be. It's been a while since she directed it at me.

Her mother marches out, leaving the painting.

But Lauryn's looking at hers again. "Is this really me? This is how you see me?"

Abbie's expression softens but her words don't. "It's how I see the relationship between us, yes. You never say anything that isn't picking at me. And it's like you've completely removed yourself from real life and real people. Like we're all non-playing characters in your little world, but we're always doing everything wrong, and your only purpose is to point it out. I honestly can't remember the last time you said anything kind—or that wasn't judgmental. It hurts *all* the time. And…I'm sorry if that hurts you or feels harsh, but I'm so worn down, I just can't anymore. I feel like I have to protect myself from you. And I understand that you're trying to do what's right, but how is constantly hurting someone right when I haven't done anything wrong to you?"

Lauryn doesn't reply. But her throat works. And still she stares at the artwork.

Abbie's tone gentles. "If *you* want to get coffee or lunch or something…I'd like to. I'd like to be closer to you again but I can't be the only one of us trying. I can't be the only one caring how the other one feels."

Her sister gives a tiny nod.

"Also…Mom is not invited."

Lauryn's mouth quirks. "Agreed," she says in a thick whisper, her voice clogged.

Uncertainly, Abbie touches the painting. "Do you want to leave this? I can get you another one."

"No. Let me…I want to look at it. And think about it."

"Okay."

"Lauryn!" Angela steps back through the open door. "Let's go. Let your sister reap what she sows—and he *will* sow, Abigail," is her prediction as Lauryn passes by her and out of the house. Angela remains to add, "You think *that* man is here because he cares about you? Think about it. His father took our house. Then the son convinced you to throw us out. It's all part of their revenge. You think he'll stay? No. He'll get you pregnant, ruin your career, and take everything you have before he abandons you—all the while congratulating himself for using a Walker woman as his whore."

"That is very near to what my father might actually think," I tell her. "It's fascinating that your mind works the same way as his."

She ignores me and hisses to Abbie, "You'll see. You'll see soon enough who is still here for you. Who will *always* be here for you."

"You're right, she will. Because I'll still be here adoring her. Respecting her. Showing her I'm so damn grateful for her. And she'll see that I'm not going anywhere."

Angela shakes her head, looking as if she's about to throw more shit at Abbie again. I get in between them and hold out her painting.

"You should probably take this. She's so damn talented, it'll be worth a fortune one day."

She sneers at me—then snatches the painting and goes. I swing the door closed behind her.

"Did…did she take it?" Abbie's got her hands over her mouth, eyes bright and watering. When I nod, she begins giggling, then covers her eyes and I'm not sure if she's laughing or crying or both.

It doesn't matter. I get my arms around her and hold her until she can breathe again. When she does, I cup her face in my hands. "All right?"

She nods but says, "Honestly, I'm not sure if I'm elated or devastated. Maybe both. Was I too harsh?"

"No."

"Not even on Lauryn? I know my mom won't change—she

probably can't change—but maybe Lauryn can?"

"Maybe. *We* went from enemies to funemies, after all."

Abbie snorts, pops up onto her toes to kiss me, then settles back with a sigh. "I guess we'll see. I think she's deeply unhappy. She might need real therapy. And if she does want to try repairing things, maybe I'll bring it up."

"It won't be easy while she's living with your mother."

"No, but…she has to make that break for herself. She has to want to make that break." She blows out a lip-buzzing breath before looking up at me. "Why am I standing here when you should be carrying me off for a victory screw?"

"Yes, ma'am," I say and haul her up over my shoulder, where she laughs and kicks her feet until I toss her onto the bed. "Do you want to be fucked or do you want me to worship you as the amazing woman you are? Wait, no. They might be the same thing."

Eyes alight, she peels off her shirt. "Are you asking whether you should treat the elation or the devastation?"

"Yeah." I help strip off her jeans. "Slow, sweet, hard, fast?"

"All of it." She pushes at my chest until I roll over. She climbs on, straddling my hips, then leaning in to brush her mouth over mine. "Thank you for not butting in."

"What?"

"I saw that you wanted to defend me. And fight for me. But just having you there was all that I needed."

"I didn't keep my mouth shut at the end."

"But you said such wonderful things, you're forgiven."

"I couldn't help myself. If your mother can't see how

fucking wonderful you are, I'll tell her." And now my heart's pounding. "It's been one year since you stopped hating me, Abbie girl. Is it too soon?"

She goes still, her gaze searching mine. Finally she whispers, "No. It's not too soon."

"Good. Because I love you. I'm in love with you. I am *so* in love with you."

"Yeah?" Her eyes glisten and she manages a watery smile. "But of course, you do. I'm vibrant. And sexy. And I am so very much in love with you."

A breath shudders from me. Holy fuck. I had no idea how that would fill me up like it just did. And what comes out of me is, "I love you so goddamn much."

She rests her forehead against mine. "So a year is not too soon?"

"Shit, no." I have to laugh. "I fell for you back at the cabin. I thought I might be, and then when you were going through those components of romantic love, I was ticking off each box. Though I'm pretty sure we didn't hit half of what makes up love, because we never even touched on how devoted I am. How loyal I'll be. And how much of my happiness is wrapped up in your hands."

She kisses me then, and it's one of those times where I don't get to say much because my mouth is too busy tasting, touching, licking—telling her without words how amazing she is. And sliding into her… Fuck. Every time is better. Yet this time, with her whispering her love into my ear as her pussy squeezes me so tight, as I come deep inside her, is the very best time.

Abbie lies atop me after. No need to get up and toss a rubber now. Not for six months. She's on birth control and neither of us is ready to think about kids, but the day she told me that we can start going bare, signaling her trust that I'll be faithful, was one of the most incredible, humbling moments of my life.

I hold her close. It's only been one year since the first time I held her. I hope to have at least a hundred years more. "It might be too soon to ask, Abbie. But when it's *not* too soon, I'm going to marry you. And then I'll put a baby in you—also when it's not too soon. Whenever you're ready."

She lifts her head to peer down at me. "Did you hit your head again?"

"Maybe. It's true that I haven't been quite right since I did. Falling in love with my enemy and all that shit."

"Then what's my excuse? You got your brains knocked by a giant branch, but I got my brains fucked out by a giant cock?"

I'm laughing too hard to kiss her properly, but goddamn, I *try*.

She's still smiling against my mouth. "Yes, by the way. To the marrying part. But I'm not changing my name to Knowles."

"We should both hyphenate. Piss everyone off." I think that over again. "That might be the worst reason to do something."

"How about this reason: You and me together, Knowles

and Walker—we're the best combination ever."

"I like that reason."

"Me, too." She looks down at me, her thumb tracing my jaw. "I thought last year was the best Christmas ever. But it might be this one, instead. Thank you."

Her voice breaks a little at the end, causing my heart to clench. "What for, Abbie girl?"

"For being you. And for loving me."

If she cries now, it's going to wreck me. "I didn't have much choice," I tell her, my voice thick. "I was a goner the moment you threatened me with that poker. I didn't realize who you were right away and thought: Harris is one lucky bastard. Then there was the first time you laughed. The first morning I woke with you in my arms. And suddenly, *I* was the lucky one."

"Lucky, yeah." Abbie exhales a shaky breath. "I know what that other component is. The one like gratitude. Remember? I couldn't think of it then. Because it's not being grateful to that person—though I am—but being grateful to the world for giving me this chance. Because so much could have gone wrong, Reed. Or gone right, actually. If I hadn't needed to escape from home. If Karilee hadn't gotten in that shower. If people had just done the right thing, I wouldn't have you now. So I feel *so* fortunate. So…"

"Blessed."

"*Yes.* To have you in my life. Knowing how easily you could have slipped right by. But you didn't." Her eyes shine. "And I got to fall in love with my best friend, instead."

Ah, fuck. I kiss her then. My heart full. And knowing for sure.

I am the luckiest bastard in the world.

THE END

Author's Note

HELLO, YOU VIBRANT AND WONDERFUL HUMAN! I hope you enjoyed *Only One Bed*—and if you want more enemies-to-lovers romance, don't miss my full-length novel *Going Nowhere Fast*, a standalone road-trip romance.

I'm writing this author note on Christmas in 2024, a day after driving over a snowy mountain pass that branches off into forest roads that inspired the location in this book. I always love writing romances set during the holiday season, and this one was no exception—although it occurred to me that I have a habit of writing holiday stories featuring a heroine with terrible parents. So to my mom and dad, if you are reading this, these terrible parental figures are definitely not based on (my) real life!

What's next? If you are an audiobook listener, I'm happy to report that the Dead Lands fantasy romance series is currently being released on audio! I also hope to finish *The Borrowed Bride* (a Dead Lands romance) followed up by *The Rubbish Bride*, which will then lead into *The Beast*, a spinoff of the Dead Lands. I also have a few contemporary standalones in mind but no firm plans for those yet. And maybe I'll give the next holiday heroines nice parents for once!

(Maybe not.)

If you'd like to be informed of my upcoming releases,

please sign up for my newsletter (katiwilde.com/newsletter). It's spam free, and I only send you an email when I have a new release, pre-order, or other important news.

I will also be signing at a few events in the summer of 2025. For information on those, please visit my website (katiwilde.com/events). I'd love to see you all in person!

And for those of you who wondered (you know who you are): Here are the lyrics for Abbie's song. I won't put the twelve verse repetitions here, just the full thing, because I think everyone knows how to sing this song from day one to day twelve.

♫*Abbie's Twelve Days of Christmas*♫

On the twelfth fuck of Christmas, my enemy gave to me:
A dozen cunts a-coming
Eleven fuckers sucking
Ten tits a-tiddling
Nine tongues a-kissing
Eight clits a-licking
Seven sperm a-swimming
Six dicks a-spurting
FIVE PUSSY EATINGS! (Hopefully not a disease!)
Four filthy words
Three fingers in
Two loads of cum
And a cock in a latex sheath!

Until next time, be kind to each other and to yourselves.
—Kati <3